The
Secret Table

Other Novels by Mark Mirsky

Thou Worm Jacob (1967)
Proceedings of the Rabble (1971)
Blue Hill Avenue (1972)

The
Secret Table

Mark J. Mirsky

Fiction Collective

Sections of this book have appeared in *Fiction, New Directions Annual 22, Tree.*

This publication is in part made possible with support from the New York State Council on the Arts

First Edition

Copyright © 1975 by Mark Mirsky
All rights reserved
Typesetting by New Hampshire Composition
Library of Congress Catalog No. 74 - 24914
ISBN: 0 - 914590 - 11 - 1 (paperback)
ISBN: 0 - 914590 - 10 - 3 (hardcover)

Published by   **FICTION COLLECTIVE**

Distributed by   *George Braziller, Inc.*
One Park Avenue
New York, N. Y. 10016

For Francis, Sheri
& Sara Russell

v.

Memory is the basis of individual personality, just as tradition is the basis of the collective personality of a people. We live in memory and by memory, and our spiritual life is simply the effort of our memory to persist, to transform itself into hope, the effort of our past to transform itself into our future.

Miguel de Unamuno

But for life itself, for memory, to have emerged from out of the wasteland of degenerating matter— the raw fact that it did, strains credulity . . . .

John Bleibtreu

Contents

Dorchester, Home and Garden

On the Tracks

There comes a rap on the door. Mrs. Chelmashibba down-stairs shouts up, "Someone to see you . . .

"Don't make him wait."

Pushing aside my books, sacred and profane, German volumes on our prophets, the psuedo-Aramaic of *Sifra di Tseniutha, Yenuka, True Detective, Eros,* pulp sheets of naked girls, I hitch my pants up over the dirty white of underwear and shuffle barefooted to the door.

I open it, undoing the latch, pushing the bolt aside, finally turning the tumbler in the lock.

The hall is dark. Mrs. Chelmashibba economizes on the lights. Her door is triple barred, terror of muggers, the neighborhood. She goes by stealth at 12 o'clock, the afternoon, scurries across the street to the iron gates of Browne's Variety, chain mail in a web across the front, boards, glass fragments stuck, spears in the plywood where the windows were. Browne peeps from the visor of his green Variety and shuffles her milk, eggs, a box of tea, fast as he can before he slams the door shut. He sees kids coming. Get back! Mrs. Chelmashibba gallops across the street, the bag bouncing in her fingers, just making it to her porch before the stones.

I escape by night, 12, slipping from the door when the babies are asleep. I slide into the alley by her house and move from yard to yard avoiding watchdogs and barbed wire, crouching in a bush by the bus stop on Talbot Ave. to leap out just before the bus glides by.

It is the last bus to the last train that will take me out of nowhere, out of childhood, into the suburbs, downtown Boston, Harvard Square, Quincy, Watertown. The long orange bulk, lighted with a thousand candlepower, slows by the shrub, the Irish driver wary, looking in shadows for assailants. I wave to him, stick my arm out of the bush.

The bus roars, picks up speed, rushes by. "Help!" I shout, leaping after it. "Help! Help!" But it disappears down the length of Talbot Ave., skipping the next stop, hurtling around the corner of Blue Hill.

Affrighted by my own nakedness I jump back between a garage and a wooden house. The gleam of gold teeth in the darkness and the razor's silent screech, the sound of footsteps—they are after me.

In a moment I am on the roof of the garage, running across the scratchy asphalt, vaulting the fence tops into the backyards of Nightingale. I hear the dogs cry, the growling of German shepherds, huskies, wolfhounds, puling of massive cocker spaniels locked in on the second floor porches. I know the moves, their fleet agility against my *chochma*. I fled this way first, eight, nine years old, pursued by the Boyle brothers, sniffing the dampness in my underwear, "Kike! Kike!"

they howled in the wind, noses thrust up like pugs, jack knives in their pockets, *schoodies* racing down the Jewish fox, driving him through cyclone netting, under the railings, hearing his high, hysterical, "Mamma!" vaulting over the last set of gray-green wooden pickets. Triumphant, they fell into a trap on the low iron palings of the synagogue, Chai Odom—a ploy now useless, the fence collapsed, but the line of ashcans beyond it still intact.

I hop, cover to cover on my tambourines, mocking my pursuit, throwing a stone to the left against the tin cover of a familiar shed, distraction, they are running on ahead, three four, five, I hear their circling in the scuffle of the leaves, dark velvet drum of their mumbo jumbo, soft deep threat in their throats, "Bam-ba-lam . . . bam-ba-lam . . ."

I am lying in an ash barrel, burrowed down deep in the soft white ghost of lumps of coal, a shroud up to my mouth and ears.

Later, before the first rips appear in the black night, tears in my curtain, certain of their patience, an hour or two at most (all predicated on this), I will dig myself out and nose home along the lintels of collapsing posts and yard sheds.

"He's waiting!" Mrs. Chelmashibba cries up again. I see the milk cartons she has left beside my door, the corrugated crate of eggs, red blood of the horseradish bottle. A smell of fish balls in the corridor and dust thick as jam over the carved oak buttons of the balustrade.

The fat Yarzheit candle throws a single skinny finger of light out on the landing. I see the cinders of my footsteps. Everyone is dead.

I stretch my hand out into darkness.

Yesterday I found myself at this hour on the railroad tracks again. A yellow *siddur* in my fist, the fraying edge of

5

the Hebrew *chumash, Exodus,* purple beside it. On my way down the tracks to New York, Miami, Argentina.

A moon arrested me, milky, awful, buttering the steel rails. Maishe, Maishe, a voice, angry and desperate.

I turn into the burning floodlight, a fly caught, my father's face, furious, panicked, tear-streaked. He grabs me by the shoulder, shaking me. "Never," he howls, "Never, Never!" I am dragged home, crying, the eyes of my friends pressed wet and gleaming against the glass window panes along Kingsdale and Warner Street, swimming like eager newts wiggling into the raw flesh of my punishment. "Never to go on them."

I have lost *Exodus* back among the cinders of the track, only a word, a step away from passing into the text forever.

It is wedged under the railbed, sturdy purple boards, the binding glue puckering up from raindrops, spilled orange sodas, hissing out of train wheels: a magical handbook that will complete my collection and so I poke for a shred of violet rag, a scrap of paper no bigger than a cigarette wrapper, stamped with Hebrew letters, a club to the boy who vanished staff in hand, on the railroad tie, heading for Codman Square.

Fleeing Egypt, Mrs. Babel of the Beth El Hebrew School, her flying blocks hurled down the aisle at his head: "Maishe! Maishe! *Shnook!*", the Boyle brothers and their pissy pants springing with mouths full of teeth, bones, knives in their knees and elbows to harry him from their burrows by the fence, his cousins the Levi boys who stood by, giggling, when the Boyles beat him, kicking his ribs on the sly while he was down, the figure of his father rising, all anger and dread as the Boyles banged his head on the splintered lip of his front steps, "What? What?", white shirt streaming out of his Daddy's pants, suspenders flapping—a broom snatched from the foyer flailing the air—Daddy chases them down Warner street, across the intersection, down their own block into the Boyle front door, the whole family fleeing down the backsteps over the railroad bed before him and he wheels, shaking the child with fury who follows him, "Your fault! Your fault!"

See where the boy flees, leaving the overseer dead, the body a lump on the track, wiped out in the rush of the Express, bearing him off past the bellowing cows of H.P. Hood & Sons milk barns, their golden calves, the piles of sweet sickly shit to . . .

He would come back to lead them all. The eldest Boyle is Pharaoh now. Only first we must get out. I sifted coal ash with my foot, crushed rock, rusting iron spike heads, chewing-gum wrapper, broken glass, tin cans, but uncovered not one shred of purple, not even a hair of colored twine.

So I am still in darkness. I feel it take hold of my fingers. At first it is no more than the draft whistling up from a crack in the downstairs door. My hand shivers in goose pimples. Then the low moan of laughter swelling in the hollow of the stairwell and now I can grasp actual flesh, its pressure gripping me, a wrestler's supple hold, but the hand has not come to throw me. The Yarzheit candle blazes like a fire and I stare into his smiling face.

"Come in," I whisper.

"There are three of us."

Yes, as I look down the stairs I see the others, one standing at the bottom of the well, the other in the middle of the steps. Their faces gleam.

"I'll fix some tea."

They hum, a murmuring that fills the hall with the light beating of bird wings.

"I have some halvah, dried out, but maybe . . . ."

Their hum thrums out my apologies.

"Come in. Come in."

"We're on our way."

"Where? Where? What's the rush?"

"Roxbury."

"You're going into Roxbury?"

"Something wrong?"

"You crazy! What for?"

They laughed.

"You'll be killed.

"Beaten."

The wings shook with thunder.

"What are you going to do there?"

"Fire!" called the one at the bottom.

"You going to set fires?"

"Watch them," they sang in chorus.

"What for?" I shook my head. The two below came floating up on the landing. The first spoke.

"What are you doing here?"-

"Looking."

"For what?"

"My . . ." I scratched my fingers in the dandruff of my scalp. "My childhood."

"Ha ha ha . . ." they leapt up and down, poking each other, merry. "You faker," one cried. "A bullshit artist," another jabbed. "What a load of crap," the third drummed. Then they all spoke in a single voice: "You smell the smoke. You taste the terror. You keep the apple under your cud."

"Look at this," cried the third, pointing to a naked girl.

"Is this the Sabbath Queen?"

They giggled.

"I . . ."

"You . . ."

"I was . . ."

"You were expecting someone else."

"Yes, yes," I cried.

"He's coming. He's coming!" The flame guttered behind me and I was suddenly in darkness.

"Fool," boomed from below.

A harsh beam struck me in the socket of my eye. The left squinting, I stared into it.

Mrs. Chelmashibba stood there, flashlight in hand, her stockings furled like sails under her kneecaps, huge slippers on her feet, the housecoat flapping from the draft of an open door.

"You promised me," I hooted down.

"*Nebbechel*!" Her bass shook the stairwell and from a shopping bag she threw them at my head, the tattered copies of my Hebrew School, *Genesis, Genesis, Genesis* . . .

They struck me in the mouth, nose chin, chest, but I clutched at them to catch so they shouldn't strike the ground, kissing, kissing their threadbare covers.

Zoo

At the corner of Kingsdale and Glenway, a double-edged Gillette, stainless steel with a platinum edge plunged in a pudding stone: it threatens whomever comes near. Yet sometimes on my way home, in the dark, I approach, put my cheek just beside the blade as I walk by, and let it tickle the stubble of my day-old beard. Aaaaaah . . . swing in, throat against the steel, my head off in one quick nod, ducking my chin, yes, over its gold glint under the lamplight.

Along Blue Hill Ave. there shines the skinny blade like an old-fashioned straight razor but so thin you can bend it between your teeth. It shimmers in the garbage cans, in the ivory tooth of the shopper, in the quick hand of the children, and the skinny toes of the teenager's black pump is edged in it. A whole avenue, a scythe in the reaper's hand.

Steel sowed in this soil, see how it glimmers in the bark of backyard oaks, slivers of it sift up in the orange grit of abandoned coal chutes, between the sidewalk cracks. One walks down the street in fear of the sharp, minute prick as the children play, cutting each other as if they were parting skin in so many kisses.

So I have encountered them in Franklin Park, ranks of blue-gray ribbon sliding up through soft puffs of their crowns, a steel pleasure garden where even the lion roars afraid, rattling his cage, and the apes cling to their rock perches, dreading the visitation of the little hunters. Knees broken by stones, the buffalo kneels in hump behind the double fence, cyclone and iron spike, rotting, his throat cut in the night by tiny marauders.

The hunt on! They sweep down the sheep's meadow from the old sage's farm, ethereal height, armed in motorcycle chain and broken bottle, zip gun and push-button knife, crouching on the golf greens, dragging the victim into the fairway ponds where, weighted, it sinks slowly to the flames of autumn leaves or the sudden flurry of the grouse.

A pair of hands lift the Ibex from its pen and set it dashing down a blocked-off road, smack on the buttock. Running, they are running behind it, beside it, before, as it veers and leaps: laughing, pulling the ribbons through their fingers, eager for the chase. The Ibex bolts up into the air, springing over their heads, over the rocks, across the gravel paths into the hollows of sand traps and, cresting for a second in silhouette at the rim of the tee for the fourth hole, bolts into the bushes where a tangle of burrs, brush, thorn branch, and trash tears its hunters; whirling round, by the high stone wall and the higher grate of the fence, it pokes and pries, dashing, zigzagging, faster and faster, working its way toward the Insane Asylum, frenzied, its hunters crying behind it, the roar of traffic down Morton Street cutting it off from the green copses of the Mount Hope cemetery; at American Legion

11

Highway it breasts the wall hoping to get into the haven of the madhouse grounds but an ancient Cadillac zooms toward it, a gleaming coffin out of Mount Hope, at eighty miles an hour over the concrete divider trying to cripple it, driving the beserk beast back into the park where it runs, runs, hearing the gun of car engines behind it, beside it, before, on the blocked-off abandoned road. It is racing on, going the round of the park faster, its lungs ripping away from their place in its chest and coming up in its throat, raw, in pieces. Hearing the elephants, lions, tigers, the lone buffalo, and the gorilla whimpering, clawing, kicking, trying to burrow under the earth.

Copley Square

It was Mrs. Chelmashibba who brought me home. She found me on the steps of the library in Copley Square. Or I was on a bench in Boston Common. Maybe I was hitching along the Jamaica Way, trying to find the ducks. She caught hold of me by the threadbare trench coat, dropping her paper shopping bags.

On the granite waves that sweep up in frozen benches to the door, an icy seat, watching the flow in and out of the library portals, I clutched my four overdue books, Spinoza, Kant, Kafka, and the *Shulhan Arukh*, hoping that Barbara Frataronne would appear in the desolate sea of pigeons and people strutting and pecking under the Copley Square's flat portico. Radishevtsky, the gravedigger, has passed through twice, mocking me. "They're looking for you, Maishe. They know those books."

I only turn my black eyes away, shivering, drawing the belt

13

in tight on my coat, the eyes have come out of the buckle holes watching for Frataronne or a sister. Witch! "Look at me!" I shout, standing up. It rings across the street to the Church. "Look!"

A dozen passers-by turn round. The cop, gay with white gloves, jerks his head from the traffic lane to see; an old man raises his umbrella but Radishevtsky, lurking in the doorway, dashes down to grab my arm, haul me forward.

"Maishe, you nut, come on. I'll treat." He drags me down the steps, around the Copley Square before the cop can register my face.

"I'll miss her," I whisper.

"Stop. Two months ago, right, the last time. Go sit in the North End at a Branch. She's through coming here. You scare her."

"*You* scared her," I scream, whacking at him. He laughs, blocking my right hand, squeezing my arm with muscles taut as iron cable, skinny thigh and elbow wrought in metal, all cog and tooth from scooping, knifing, gouging the frost-bitten ground at Mount Hope, New Calvary. Radishevtsky whose shovel bites through November, December, January, delighted to be breaking in on worms, a trick he learned at Buchenwald, an honest trade. He, a lover of Schopenhauer, liked to spit on the famous, hack in their faces, strut on tuxedo and gown, mangle private parts. He knows everyone Governor to the Mayor. Your mother too, he told me once, knocked on her door, let her in on a few things.

"Come on, eat up your apple. Vanilla ice cream too. Piping hot. The girl was nothing. No sense of humor. A *shicksa* too. 'Women,' said Schopenhauer . . ."

" 'Exist for the propogation of the race,' " I jumped his mouth. "Radishevtsky, your lines are dead as your customers. Both stink. Dig down six feet! Think you're in Plato's cave? A scratch is what you and your philosophy are good for, an itch in the *touchus*, that's comfort?"

Radishevtsky grins, a big, wide tooth-shattering spread, black stumps into thin blue lips. He picks his nose with pleasure. "Maishe, you're O.K. You're beginning . . . Practice, you'll be ready for the Father." He reaches out and tugs my cheek, "Good."

I haven't forgiven. Are hot green apples under Bickford's cardboard crust, a glass of homogenized, compensation for Frataronne's fat little tits and the broad Italian ass chafing her green skirt of corduroy? She was blown into my arms four weeks ago, a gust sweeping around the corner of Copley knocked her books, tits, purse, into me and as I stooped to help, I saw the hem of slip, line of calves, a second with her upper thighs. I fitted that kicked-off loafer back to her foot and kneeling in the granite crib, looked up into mocking black eyes: "What are you reading?"

I knew already from the plastic covers of the library books I caught cartwheeling down the steps, *Walter on Wednesday, Sixteen and Softness, April Dreams,* but one, red-grained cloth, gold-stamped, I held back, snatched as it was about to leap like a spark into the gutter, concealed behind my back, and I drew it forth as she spoke, "Junk."

That explosion on her small red lips, the tiny fuzz of a Neapolitan moustache like the stroke of a light eyebrow pencil on her upper: soft olive face puckering in self-disdain.

"Plato?" I asked.

"It's a high-school assignment." I caught the pink strands of gum, sticky confectionery strung her white teeth.

"You are a cave dweller."

"What?" Her brow wrinkled, the gum a love bead between

15

her lips.

"You don't know about Plato's cavern?"

"I didn't get that far."

"Are you returning it?"

"Yeah."

"Oh, you have to read that first."

"What's in the cave?"

I lowered my voice, "Shadows."

"What's so hot about that?"

"Look," I whispered, reaching up suddenly to grasp her hand, firm child's flesh. "This is not real, this is shadow. In the Cave I could touch you, an image of you, the divine form which you are struck from."

"Wow, you're weird," she giggled.

"What's your name?"

"Barbara," she answered, letting here eyelashes flicker.

"Come on and have a cup of coffee with me."

"O.K." She took the gum out of her mouth and stuck it to the red cover of Plato, sealed it with her thumb.

We clatter down the Copley Square steps. I hope my socks do not smell and pull in the flap of the trench coat to hide the gravy stains on the front and collar of my white shirt.

"Barbara what?"

As she speaks her last name I try to summon up a line of Dante, Petrarch, but only Greek flashes in translation. "I've seen your face before."

"Cut it out," puckering her cheek.

"No, Plato says that when we behold a face of real beauty, a kind of shuddering comes over us because we recognize with awe an old reality. Look, I'm shivering!" I reach out again, take her hand, holding it as we walk. She does not reject it.

"I know where you've seen me."

"Where?"

"In that cave."

"Ah," I cry and swing around to kiss her on the cheek. "I'm not afraid. Look," I fall down on the sidewalk, scattering pigeons, "I worship you," not letting her hand go so she almost ducks down with me but I am up, skipping, arm in arm with my goddess to the Bickford.

Has she read this? That? No? I construct a book list for her. I enroll her in college. She will teach, support me as a writer. How is her high school? Awful, the nuns are narrow? Wonderful, the girl is in revolt. Reckless, I deprecate the Rabbis, narrow too. We will make our own tradition, pan-Mediterranean, all sun and ocean. I taste the sea breeze over Boston; it salts her cheek. I almost bite the tawny dimple.

On to the Bickford!

And there I illuminate the glass counters, plastic tables, seats of leatherette, with light, wipe out the tawdry yellow of Edison bulbs and tubes with the white brilliance of Hellas, all surfaces are creamy marble running with a single rosy streak, a stream of joy. Barbara and I are touching fingers, tributaries. I squeeze her lemon slice, she shovels sugar to my cup, babbles of her school in East Boston, and I see myself climbing the wooden steps with books under the approving eye of her mustachioed uncles, grandfathers, organ grinder's monkeys hopping on the stairs, the white embroidered bridal coverlets are spread out in the master bedroom for our consummation, her mother crooning love songs in the closet as Frataronne undoes her clasps and summons me to brown breasts, fags of nipples, a dusky volcano between her legs, perfume of ash on her hairs, we faint away in glowing love,

17

hunks of rock and fire, Stromboli! Stromboli!

Dazed, holding hands on the Bickford table, I smelled the sulphur harsh as gunpowder, the stink of rotting eggs, un-washed armpits, "Maishe? What's the story! Baby-sitting?"

Radishevtsky, plucking at a hairless Van Dyke, plumps himself into an empty chair and scrapes it across the tiles, wedging in beside us.

I can feel the tremor through Miss Frataronne.

"Maidle, Maidle, what are you talking about?"

"Plato!" I cut in, desperate to shove him off.

"Ooooh," whistled Radishevtsky, pursing his lips. "What do you think of him?" He laid his bony hand on Barbara's. She pulled her own away, down into her lap.

"He's very nice."

"Plato nice, mmmmm?"

Frataronne said nothing.

"What's nice about him?" Radishevtsky's voice had the uncanny cutting edge that got under the skin and pricked, sandpaper in your ear drums. "You forgot so quick?" He picked up the copy of Plato and thumbed the pages. "You got any idea what's inside?"

"He's cute."

"Plato is cute."

"He's cute," she said, pointing to me.

"Oh, we're talking about him. It's not such a literary dis-cussion."

Barbara got up. "I have to go."

"Wait," I said, "I'll walk you."

"No," she was gathering her books.

"Just to the subway."

"No."

But I had jumped up and was sprinting along beside her.

18

"Don't mind him. He's a nut. Works in a cemetery."

"I like him. He's funny."

"Look, when will I see you?"

"Tomorrow or the next day."

"Where?"

"The library."

"Tomorrow. Make it tomorrow."

"O.K."

"What time?"

"Same time."

"O.K., it's a date, right?"

"Right!"

"Want me to go home with you?"

"No, not today."

"O.K. Hey . . ." we had reached the subway entrance. "I love you!"

She laughed, blushing, and ducked down into the tunnel.

Wheeling around, I smelled my musty underwear. In a store window I caught sight of my collar, soiled and torn. I had to clean up, shave, buy some socks and I had only one touch, back in the Bickford, Radishevtsky.

"A mental myopic," he cackled as I slid in beside him.

"Listen, I need a few bucks."

"What for?"

"Forget it!" I shoved the table into his stomach, bolting up.

"Wait a minute. So hot under the collar," his hand caught my wrist and dragged me down. "I know what you're up to. Some razor blades, a new shirt, maybe a dab of eau de cologne, eh?" With his free hand he reached into a back pocket and drew out a battered brown wallet. "Take a walk through Filene's, you can get a few free squirts off the counter." He

19

scooped out one torn twenty dollar bill crinkled like an oak leaf and stuffed it into my hand still pinioned by his wrist pin to the table. "Wonderful, what the *potz* will do, sex drive. For your own sainted mother you wouldn't brush your teeth. Now comes a squat little dummy and you anoint yourself with oil. Go!" he cried, releasing and waving me on. "Spit on Radishevtsky. Your days are numbered too. You're no more twenty-two."

"Thanks," I blurted, trying to shake his hand.

"Naaah," he whacked it away. "No bullshit, please. I'm paying for entertainment."

*   *   *

There is snow on my shoulders. I'm sitting in shiny black pumps, paper thin soles, the two dollar special at Morgan Memorial oozing shoe polish from the cracks in the leather. A new shirt, the soft cotton bead of Woolworth's, and thick black woolen socks with a fresh elastic band snapping when I put them on, sliding the new pants out of Filene's Basement over them, still reeking of cologne from their upstairs counters, a hasty squeeze before the white-haired counter women eye me and wave me off with huffing. I'm sitting in the scent of *April's Showers* dreaming of Barbara who comes up the steps of Copley Square to take my hand and lead me on into the lobby where the marble lions are roaring for us, outstretching their matted paws to hug our flesh, smacking their chiseled teeth, lapping bosoms, breasts, buttocks, licking us clean of clothes; skin, bone, and hair we crouch in a corner of the courtyard and, under an icy drift, lock in love like statuary. Barbara's body tawny as a lioness, her breath steaming in my mouth, my finger tickling her tailbone, nuzzling her ear so

20

that she shivers and trembles with pleasure as I whisper of Aesop.

Green grass under the snow and crocuses lurking in green shafts, nubs sprung to push at the first blush of warmth, April shoots in every crack of us, diddled by a host of dandelion stalks, ferns lashing our posteriors, the courtyard seething like a Shawmut Ave. back lot in July, tropical undergrowth crosses with the seedings of the Library matrons, Indian vines wind about us, her breasts sprout into long yellow squash, her behind into a grand orange pumpkin, and my stick is gold, crimson, black, and blue, a pole of colored corn. Barbara, all Boston is coming to fruit!

A white flurry over our heads. More and more, a blizzard now of icy scraps, fat as thumbs, long as fingers. From the upper windows of the courtyard a silvery rime falling off the windowsills, the ancient librarians poking their heads out, powdery hair, shower us with filing cards torn up into wedding bouquets, the Dewey decimal system is falling, gathering in great heaps and drifts in our yard. "Barbara," I call. She is slipping from my grasp, her thighs wiggling away in the stack of confetti burying us, "Barbara!"

I grab for her leg but only catch a piece of paper. The cackle of the old lady librarians shakes the pile. Barbara is rising into the sky of Copley Square in the snow storm; confetti, clinging in long, long trails to her body, a dazzling wedding dress. She is weeping tears of happiness. I clutch only a flake of Dewey.

"Read," she calls, her tears little scraps of white.

It is the name. I am weeping too as I look down. It is the book. I have found it at last, flung out of a drawer of the catalogue, the parchment crackling in my hand, its Hebrew characters embossed in black Assyrian script, the English

21

transliteration below, light streaming from the index.

I see the letters combine themselves! I grasp black balls of the vowels. I am drawn upward into closing and opening consonants coming apart in letters, millions, millions, spilling out the secret. I am being spoken, wholly, wholly, wholly.

Hallways

Almost all of them have been carried off. They died in stairwells and leaning against doorjambs, in stained petticoats, soiled underwear; huge creatures, a race of giantesses, two hundred, three hundred pounds, but of soft, flaccid flesh, bulky and almost unmovable until the end when the final wasting set in and the fat bubbled off them leaving only a few charred bones for the undertaker after the Angel's fire.

The old men, torn trousers and shirt collars in shreds collapsed on the street with heart attacks, fell babbling blood into the gutter, stomach ulcers split. Met the whirling sword and shook their chicken wings, frail elbows, wrists flapping; went under cursing. Sacks of giblets He hauls away on His back, screeching. The windows clucking softly, half out of their apartments in the hallways as downstairs they board up the windows, nail shut the door, cut the telephone electric wires while the old lady stares into the dust, moving her rags over the jamb, cleaning, cleaning against the inevitable day.

Pestilence, they are swelling in doorways all over Dorchester, old ladies in smelly dresses, soiling themselves, incontinent, blown up with plague they burst the jambs; lift their flyspecked ceilings. Temples are trembling and all Boston turns, breaks its stride, looks up at rooftops, beams, stones, sliding down upon it.

Overhead the sun is rolling, and tumbling after it moon and stars: pell-mell through the black sky. The old ladies stiffen, feeling the tug in their stocky calves yet fastened to the doorjambs, waiting for a world that cannot stop to right itself, muttering childhood songs into empty hallways.

Then they begin to cry together, the eighty-year-old ladies on the top floors of the Dorchester three deckers begin to weep, quietly, tiny tears trickling down their noses, a terrible sound which rattles the nails in their window boards, bolts across their porches, rising above the honking of the traffic on the Avenue, shouting of the children in their front yards, barking of dogs; and each man, woman, child, rushing to and fro below suddenly hears a thrilling in the ear, arrested; the policeman thinks of sirens, squad cars, the fire chief reaching for his axe, ready to assemble poles, hoses, masks. Even the little hoodlums in the street feel for razors, zip guns, imagining they might come to the aid of abandoned belligerents, leap athwart the porches with steel.

Then they flee, dogs, children, policemen, firemen, murderers. They are running away, harder and harder, puffing, chests tight, putting as many miles as they can between themselves and the dusty top floors. Never, never, looking back.

Midnight

I was on my way to demand an answer from the sage, the great scholar in Brookline. Yes, I had imagined how I would interrupt his lesson on the subtleties of the snake, flinging, on the long table of the three hundred disciples who gathered to wonder at his wisdom and story telling, a bag, a plain blue-and-white-striped laundry sack just such as my mother used to have in her back hall but filled with the soiled underwear of the old ladies of Dorchester. Stretch the canopy of the heavens from this?

I was on my way, I swear, walking, starting from Talbot Ave., as the sun went down, the bag on my back, walking through the storm, laughing, a smile on my face, happy, singing. He will have an answer, answer. All around me the world bursting into brilliance, white, crystal, everything in sight, black rooftops, asphalt road, trash, ash cans, even the laundry on my back, bleached, a condensed, wonderous white, and I

walked crying into hallways of purity.
  "Dancing in the moonlight . . . ."

The Three Muses Meet Isaiah

So, Mrs. Chelmashibba found me, dug my body out from under the snowdrifts on the steps of the Copley Square or tore my frost-hard fingers from the lower branches of the oak on the Jamaicaway.

She brought the body back. Whether as one frozen limb encased in ice, a pink fossil in a green transparent block; or several pieces broken apart where the weight of snow had snapped it; fragments, a million ruby vessels, diamond chips, bone exploded by the cold, scooped into her ragged pockets; she collected me in brown paper shopping bags, brought me home to Dorchester, knit me together in the vast damp bed of her widowhood, the comforters she had stitched wet with the steam of my flesh as she gave me her secret heat, hugging my body, calling out prayers and nursing me till I quickened and the healing flush went through my patched-together soul.

I awoke a boy, smelling the sour reproach under me in the

mattresses. Seeing Mrs. Chelmashibba shaking her head above, wagging her thick finger, Shame! Shame!

I rose scalded in her eyes, my body red with heat, embarrassment, to learn my lessons. Her rough hands washing me in the scarred white tub, thumping the breath back in my body, slipping fresh flannel underwear over the angry chapped skin of my crotch, pulling the patched corduroys, cotton shirt over my legs and head, capping me with a black skull piece, taking me by the hand upstairs to the room where my utensils lay; fat block of India rubber, polished wood ruler with a steel ribbon in its heart, orange-brown notebooks with neat blue lines: the empty shelves awaiting my library.

And Mrs. Chelmashibba fills the room with strong Russian tea that smells of Tartar saddles, clotted with a jam of wild cherry husks, tiny bows of dough, light and hollow, girls' wings sprinkled with sugar flakes. Her body is an enormous *challah*, white bread colored with egg yolk. Crisp and fragrant it rises above me. Honey runs from the spigots of her breasts, drips across my mouth. Drowsy, I slump on the desk, rocking swaddled in the warmth of the oven. Twisted in the braids of holy bread, climbing their ladder back into the milky haven of the angel's bosom.

And now, no more than a dot, creeping along the blue line of the empty notebooks, ink streaming from my fingernails as I scratch them on the pages, crawling from margin to margin, blotting mistakes with my clean white cotton underwear, I begin my work: *The Chronicle History of Dorchester*, appendices on Roxbury and Mattapan. The sun is lighting up the space between the two azure bars as I swing in them, happily tracking my black hand and footprints over the paper tinted with gold. Oh hear the voices singing, choruses of Ophanim and holy Chayoth and Seraphim rushing back and forth over my head, exclaiming with delight, make much of the mess I leave behind. And below me the three muses are waving: one black and comely, she calls to me.

"I guhtta hug dis liddle creeper. I guhtta squeeze dat boy. M m m m m m m . . . Mommy's liddle mo-lass-es pie. Mmmmm . . . I guhtta chew dat liddle chee-eek." She opens her laughing mouth and it's all ivory and gold, tickling my ear with her tongue, filling it with hot dark caramel, rolling and shaking her little behind, for me, hugging the high-busting taffy apples of her tits, my face is sticky with sugar. She croons, "Now don' you lah, ah wan to heah it from de *soul*, big ole puff, take dat cotton battin out yoah mowf, tell how sweet yoah mammy is!" And she squeezed me until the ink spurted up through my cheeks and my toes turned blue black.

"Ah'm tryin' not to mumble, Mammy," I squeaked out. She shrieked and giggled, shook me up and down, back and forth she shimmied with me in her bosom until every bone and socket was shivered out of place, slipping her long fingernails into the latchets of my muscles, unstringing, unzipping, doubling, and tripling my joints, till I was so loose I swayed like a puppet and she swung me out letting the long blue fox stoll along her shoulders bark and yap to the *Lindy,* the *Boogaloo*, the *Dirty Guinea*, the *Nasty, Bellyrub, Double Dong.* I was rollin', rockin', and weevilin', mah mowf wide open wid, "Annie had a bay bee/ Can' wohk no moah!"

"*Vas machtah,*" cried the second muse, snatching me into her embrace as I doubled back for a final twist to the floor, scraping the back of my head and buttocks, "What's this?"

"Mammy," I called. "I jes got to do / dee Boo-ga-loooo."

"*F'arshemen on dis mishiguss mit Mammy,*" she exclaimed, seizing my whirling body, stuffing me upside down

29

between her olive breasts, rolling and grinding me against a powdery stomach and soft mammaries. "You got to take pain, *tsurris*!" She struck herself hard in the chest. I gagged on the rubbery peg of her mill. She whacked herself again. "*Tsurris*!" And the spiggot began to flow. I was choking on rich cream, butter, a limpid stream of Farmer's cheese.

"Enough with the dairy, Ma!"

"Maishelle, Maishelle," she wept, plucking me up, dripping milk. "My little *pishekeh*, here's a kiss and here's a smack." She cracked me and bussed me until my head rang with affection. "*Tsurris*," she wept, letting me drop to the stage draped with blue-checked oil cloth like a kitchen table which she beat on with an outsized cake roller, smashing at my tiny toes. "*Shandeh* and a *Charpeh*! Oy!" And her tears drenched me, each drop a barrelful but not bitter, sweet, cloying, and tasty, a liquor of apricot, peach, plum, I licked it from my fingers and hands, scooped it from the shiny surface under me where it oozed and dripped; the rainbows in the fruit trees burst around my head and I saw my mother not crying but shaking her head.

"Mother, I'm sorry, Mother." Her black hair twisted into braids and she looked like a schoolgirl. The belly was swollen under her dress.

"Look," she said, picking the hem up.

"No," I screamed. "No." For she was dying.

"That's your lesson. Learn it."

And I looked away until she was gone. Stood without hope.

A third hand stole into mine. It was the last muse and of her I cannot say clearly, was she Irish, English, Scotch, for a time it seemed as if her hair was copper, then fiery red, soft silver-blonde. On the corner of Kingsdale she sits in her chair, a blanket over her knees, a face so smooth and white, angelic calm, a fairy princess.

It is she who held my hand and told me, sing of *sadness*, the unspoken grief she twists into a smile out of wasted legs she can no longer run on, such peace in her face, why we can almost see the halo floating over her Gothic golden hair and we know she has something strange to tell us but our mothers have warned us to leave her alone for she has a sickness. Even the touch of her fingers! Polio! Infantile paralysis.

How many times I passed her stone-pillared porch, her slight body like flotsam above the huge granite blocks, and looked up to see her smiling but not at me, the whole street, at Dorchester; now I feel her tender girl's flesh, cool and moist in my hand, and the disease comes fluttering up to my chest. I am paralyzed with horror at my own body, appetite, on my lips her ghastly, beautiful smile, sadness. Yes it is the sound of my own English, a tongue of melancholy and reserve, sweet with reticence.

And the fourth who cannot come, the smirking berry-fleshed vixen who I sought in the holes of our back yard, under the sticky leaf of the skunk cabbage and crotches of our pear trees, shooting shafts of love to her out of the broken hedges down Warner Street, tracking her through the bushes of abandoned lots, the musk of her in the first purple violets hidden under a rotting telephone pole felled between our house and the neighbor's and the riot of yellow dandelions up and down the block lawns; only her echo, Massachusetts, Woonsocket, Squantum, Shawmut, Pawtucket, Nantasket, Neponset, rattling of pumpkin seeds and the bumping of the wind against the hill's trees, Mattapan!

Black, blonde, auburn, straight and curly, their tresses cloak me in the twists of Mrs. Chelmashibba's *challah* as I make my way over and under the lines of my history. "Sing me hwaethwugu."

"Hwaet sceal ic singan?"

"Sing me frumsceaft."

How it was all farm, fallow soil and dung, vast sheepscote and salt marsh, the resort of wolves, bears, rattlesnakes, ". . . a frontier Town pleasantly seated, and of large extent into the main land, well watered with two small Rivers, her body and wings filled somewhat thick with houses to the number of two hundred and more beautiful with fair Orchards and Gardens, having also plenty of Corn land and store of Cattle, counted the greatest Town heretofore in New England." Ay Dorchester! What have I to do with thee? It is not of ministers I sing, Maverick, Mather, or congregants, "Mr. Ambrose Martin, For calling the Church Covenant a stinking carrion, and a human invention, and saying he wondered at God's patience, feared it would end in sharp, and said the ministers did dethrone Christ and set up themselves. Fined ten pounds." Nor Chickatabot or Cutshumaquin, descendants trailing toward the graveyard at Neponset's mouth, wailing where the tide lapped the river waters. Nay, still my land lay waste and pasture until the Hebrews poured out of burning Chelsea, its rag factories, clutching their bags of remnants, swarmed over Clark's Farm and Franklin's Field. Now lift the harp. Spread the tent stave to the right and left, three deckers clapped up in clusters, unnumbered as the stars. Now sing of mighty men, *Hindedikehs, Blindehs, Stummers, Pickavaters, Goniffs, Grobbers, Leidigeers, Paskudnaks*: there arose on the Avenue that processed to the great Blue Hill, the giant *Krumers*, massive dwarfs who bowled over walking with their heads touching the ground. What string can stand the monstrous strain of Bolishevsky, the blacksmith, who threw

32

up factories for iron, steel? Bang instead the anvil for this *Shtakah* who came limping from Pinsk, his forge tied to his back, blowing on coals until he was black in the face, smoke out of his ears, in later years, a gentleman, a *Killowater*, his hernia trussed in a platinum girdle as he sold lots up and down Calendar, Woodrow, Blue Hill, and put up a synagogue for Jacob to recite his glory.

Stretch yourself against the loom and with your fingers in the warp and woof of shuttles, pluck, pluck a song to the princes, the Nabbi of Cotton, the Gaon of Woolen, the King of Essex Street. Did these men not live among us? Drawing a web of dry goods toward Dorchester so that the seconds of Lowell, Lawrence, Manchester carpeted our streets, swaths of worsted up and down the crude wooden stairs of Hosmer and Nightingale: the whole district in snipping, cutting, sewing pressing, packaging, peddling; bolts of good stuff, cheap stuff, fluttering over our heads from Roxbury to Mattapan. Under its shadow banks spring up, loan associations, accountants.

Out of the way Honorable Ancient Artillery Company— the regiments of Blue Hill Ave. are marching by, ranks of door-to-door men, retailers, pharmacists, dentists, doctors, lawyers. See what the rag pile of Chelsea bred.

My *zaide*, the Flower Prince, whose stalls in the wholesale market were poetry, plush red with the Hadley Rose, pink frill of the frosty Massachusetts carnation, tight syrupy buds, bulbs of Poeticus, King Alfred jonquils, white with Callas lillies, butter yellow, blue with Tin Gentian: weep over his disastrous corner of gladiolas that descended in boxes, crates, car loads, trains filled with those flowering *lulavs* he'd promised to buy until he had to plant all Dorchester in them, cover it in blossoms like the plain of Sharon, stuffing them into every available wedding, bar-mitzvah, funeral, until the poorest cold-water flat bloomed with the opulence of Gardiner's Palace.

Here are the furriers head to toe in mink, sable, the least of them in muskrat and beaver, seal, silver fox, black Persian lamb; a whole tribe of Tsars. Now come the junkmen, justly famous in old manuscripts, whose piles are better than the fine gold, whose tin sparkles like silver, sweeping pearls and emeralds from the gutter, coining the dust. Joining their efforts with lumbermen, hewing out concrete blocks, a cistern for the living waters.

See, there are our boys, mocking the Atlantic & Pacific. Bidding the waves of grocery to stop and shop. Our sons draw honey from the rock, it drips down their shelves with the fat of wheat. Wonder bread. We grow. We prosper. Now God, stand up for Dorchester!

Here come the heroes, marching out in front!

See the *baleboss*, running, see, in front of that one, fawning, a *toches leker*. Right down before their *chochem*, they can't bend the knee or bow the head enough. A genius!

K. K. Wish, the lawyer who stole for himself half of West Roxbury, Roslindale, all the Jewish burial lands that should have supported the poverty stricken synagogues of Dorchester, buying off their boards for a few pennies so that funds had to be squeezed from the poor, the aged, the children of the Hebrew School. And he didn't even give them a hippopotamus for their money like Simcha.

Simcha, fabulous tribune of the people who purchased Leviathan for the glory of Dorchester, Mattapan and Roxbury, marched it down Blue Hill Avenue collecting coppers from the kiddies. Simcha, who did not stand by when the massive beast, last of a long line, sickened in the tiny pen

34

allotted to it at the Franklin Park Zoo, a concrete crib just large enough for it to make a half turn in a quarter of a circle as it rose on a tiny ledge above the fetid waters, slimy with sewage in which it steeped, gangrene like sorrow soaking through its thick grey hide, in its narrow captivity sodden unto death.

Five! Five hippos dead. And even the *sadists* on the City Council, their fingers wet with soft green kickbacks from the Park Commisioner relented and compassionate cried, enough.

"No more hippos!"

"No more hippothh?" Simcha had anticipated the promised end, jumping to Africa, Dorchester to Africa on one leg, straddling continents, cornered the hippo market. Behemoth was packed, crated, on its way for the sticky-fingered kids of Dorchester, their streamers, windmills, carmel candy, Cracker Jacks boxes. Simcha would be first, on the spot, with a hippo.

"No hippos."

"I bought it alweady!"

Little tears trickled from the eyes of his fellow Councillors, tiny drops ran down their noses as they struggled, squeezing their lips and cheeks, but it tickled the soft skin on the undersides of their toes, those hairy monsters of crime and corruption, glee, and at last they roared, howled, hee-hawed, slapped each other on the back and hiccupped for pure pleasure as they proclaimed, "Too bad." "What a mis-

---

Flowers: from *A Natural History of Dorchester, Mattapan & Roxbury*.

There are the dead blooms scattered over the neat slabs of the New Calvary and Mount Hope Cemetery, acres of cut

take." "Oooh, you made a boo-boo." "Better take care of it." "How much did it cost?" "What does it eat a day?", as they lowered the boom, 4 tons of masticating hippo, crated in a large expensive box, to be fed, hosed down, petted, under the watchful eye of the Society for the Prevention of Cruelty to Animals, on Simcha's head. Bang!

Right down on the South Boston docks it came and Simcha was so staggered he didn't wake up for two days to the huge grey snout deep in the empty lining of his wrinkled blue-serge suit. The hippo was eating out of his pocket, fifty dollars a day.

Simcha! Simcha! A smaller man would have gone to the bottom of the Bay with the hippo on top of him. Is a man a dog, an elephant, to have his rear poked at by trainers? Would Simcha be stood up on his hind legs, his privy parts in a ludicrous show all over Boston?

He knew who the clown was. No mooning by the seaside with a sad amphibian. Simcha hitched a collar to the beast, smacked its *toches* and set out for Dorchester. "A pawade!"

"Pawade!" he cried, pushing, pulling, prodding the hippo into its first steps across the continent. A host of Talbot Ave.

---

blossoms withered to straw, blossoms that you could have had fresh but a few hours from the best florists in Boston merely by scrambling under the cemetery fence through the dog hole below the wire, or quickly hopping over the easy vault of the stone wall. Yet no table in our streets was adorned with these trimmings. They had been touched by the hand under the grass and were stuck fast to their stone chips. Only the wind moved them at will, blowing petals loose over the green lawns and whole bouquets still bound by their rubber bands, tight-fisted. Yet on Mother's Day I went down to the graveyard fence where the lilac bushes sprang wild from the edge, once farmstead, no homeowner to protest my fingers' stripping. Here, the barren graveyard, all short-cropped lawn and institutional green hedge seemed to pour its violet sorrow, surging up in lilac shrubs so deep in purple the air swam with perfume and the insects buzzed as if blood were misting where the bushes shed their petals into my arms. Basketfuls I gathered and carried to my mother's bed, pushing open the door to the room where she lay raveled in white sheets, smiling and I filled the chamber with the scent of my birth, her death.

Tulips, rising in a border along the old ruddy brick of the Sarah Greenwood Elementary School, the wax of deep red, cream, yellow, egg white, like chewy bouquets of our kindergarten crayons, color so thick each April it drips on our fingers in the warmth of the sunny afternoon and the luster of rainbows melted in my mouth. See, they tip their cups and I drink, brush the chocolate brick of the wall with the fuzz of the honeybee, curling in the mint of ivy leaves, wet and unfolding, buzzing, distilling each moment into my eternity.

Trumpets of the Morning Glories, blue horn clear and sharp by the side of our gray porch, my mother's finger pointed them out holding the notes of the early morning sunlight and warned me away from the bush full of black berries, poisonous, a mouthful of their lavender, death, squished into our mud pies and muffins. And the bleeding cherry tree next door which bloomed and bore, hysterical fecundity, so many white blossoms, so many hard red buttons, its bark crackling and oozing fistfuls of sap, heavy as glue, like the face of its

37

owner, a terrible cherry birth mark running down half his face into his shirt collar, sweating knobs and seams of scarlet flesh, dripping insides. I put my thumb in the soft goo of the tree's heart where it swelled from a crack in the branch, sticking my teeth into the mucilage of cherries, trying to taste the sugar of the tree's fire, angry tissue of its soul bubbling up from some hot spring, as birds carried off the ripe bursts of wine.

I felt flesh in the craggy bark of the backyard oak tree, thick as a house, shedding acorns like a waterfall, its roots deep into a cold brittle stream of shell and meat under the crust of the earth, breeding squirrels in families and tribes through its branches and over the roofs of surrounding houses, its ancient knees rising bone and scar out of thin grass, leaves shaken loose, leaning back against our neighbor's garage that a nudge would crack, shiver to pieces of concrete block.

Older than Dorchester perhaps, its bole in the hold of an Indian pouch, a sprout of Abraham's terebinth. Two pear trees grew at a distance, their bark a smooth, girlish texture, yet one year they leafed barren, no more showers of mouth-puckering sickles. I was bitter at them barren, maiden aunts, they spread their branches to no purpose. My vineyard was dead. No more gangs of other streets appearing suddenly over the top of our masonry wall, rocks in hand to stone me into my back hallway while they aimed to knock the fruit into their hats and paper bags or clambered, squirrels, into the upper branches, shaking, while I screamed for mother, threatening to shoot with a beebee gun. No bottles of soft green slabs, sweetmeat cooked for the fruitless months of Febru-

Perizzites were beating the bushes, whacking on packing cases, screaming Yiddish obscenity, trying to goad Simcha's pet into a trot. It was Hippo Day down Blue Hill Ave.; Simcha with a cashbox lifted from the Eggleston-to-Mattapan-Square trolley slung around his midriff over the shiny tuxedo, considerably frayed from his efforts at shoving, the midnight blue beshat at the cuffs and elbows, strutting in front, his hands out for pennies.

"A hippo! A hippo for the kidd-eethh!" He shook the wire cage of his M.T.A. Tsodokkah box as children cheered him on, his bully boys pulling and tugging on the animal, trying to keep it from kicking in fenders on the parked cars, scrambling under its oversized hooves for the occasional penny, lead slug, some thiriftless Dorchester mother put into her baby's hand.

Simcha mounts the Hippo's head at the G&G Delicatessen in front of flashbulbs and reporters swimming in a warm tepid bath of attention, trying to restrain the beast who is snorting after the cornbeef sandwiches inside; declaiming on *Anti-Semitism & The Hippopotomus*. Simcha who sold City Hall, The State House, Jerusalem, to his constituents. And he was working on bigger things. If only our district had turned Black sooner! He could have sold them Africa.

"Shit!" A crowd of Ophanim swoop down. "Stop this!" the holy Chayiim are screaming. "Is this worth singing over?" cry the outraged Seraphim.

---

ary, December, March, the kitchen steaming with orchard blooming. My father smiled at the sterile limbs. He had placed a curse on the nuisance of life, sprouting out of his fingers, inscrutable, our backyard dead. My sister was the last living thing out of our cornucopia.

Why do you interfere? You angels are ignorant of man.

"All right, we admit it, but who can help overhearing? You promised us psalms. Is this the music of Dorchester?" The angelic host dropped their pants. With gilded buttocks began to hiss.

Mrs. Chelmashibba! Mrs. Chelmashibba! Help me. Tell them it's true. I'm not making it up.

Chayiim, Ophaniim, Seraphim burst into titters. "Listen *kuni-lemel*," a big golden one says, "Who cares if it's true or false? Is it nice?"

Mrs. Chelmashibba!

"Forget Mrs. Chelmashibba," a silver Chayiim chirps. "She's gone. Packed her bags and hit the trail for Quincy. Look out your window!"

I pull on the cord of the window shade and let the yellow parchment creep up an inch or two.

No!

There it lies, the straw, not just broken in two, like the back it collapsed, but singed, a black ash from top to bottom. Mrs. Chelmashibba's pipe is twisted out of shape, the grates crowbarred off, the windows busted, electrical wires like a fistful of veins dangling loose in the air. Browne's Variety has been robbed and burned.

"Better get going," a girlish Seraph teases, flapping back and forth, making the window shade flutter.

My books?

"Your books?" mock the angels. "It's the same old story. You know it by heart. You recite it to everyone you meet. Who's listening?"

Later . . .

"Oooo," the angels whistle, "Thinks he's Isaiah."

But . . .

"There's nothing downstairs. Not an old matzoh ball. While you're dreaming, the old lady tucked away every crumb and stick into her crates, paper bags, steamer trunk. Maishe, the house is *Peysachdikeh.* You're speaking to the Angel of Death. The kids are waiting outside under the hedges, in the cellar holes, the yard across the way, a box of matches and a can of kerosene. I'm going to rub my behind on the Lally column under the back porch, brimstone, this house is a torch. Listen!"

The wings stop. In the silence I hear the small still sound, a scratch, and faint scent of sulphur, a curse. "Sheet!" Another scratch.

"It didn't catch, Maishe, git!"

I rush to the door. It is nailed shut. Below, the snap and crackle of the first flames sing out. Wheeling I turn on the angels. How?

"Your *tzitssis*, quick!"

Where are they?

"Under the bed."

I run to the door again, hammer on it. No one can hear. The angels are dim in the room. The fire under the porch begins to roar. Smoke is curling through the keyhole. I get down on my knees and crawl under the huge double bed Mrs. Chelmashibba has given me. In the middle, below the stalactites of sagging stuffing by the silver glow of the host, I see my blue *taliss* bag clotted with dust. Tearing open the catches I pull out a heavy white cotton banded with black, my grandfather's shawl.

"The *tfillin* too," voices cry.

I fumble with the paper crowns on the polished ebony phalacteries. "Wrap yourself up."

Crouching, I roll and twist, wrapping the mantle around

41

me, slipping the leather straps in circles on my forearms, choking on dust and flying cinders. "Hurry!"

I slide out from under the bed, stand up, squint through clouds of grey soot, heat stinging my bare feet. "The window!"

I can't. It's two stories.

"Fly."

They sweep me in their wings through the glass panes, wood struts, my forehead bloodied, the black straps on my left arm clamping a severed artery tight after I put my fist into the transparent mirror and burst in one leap into the bushes. I stand up shaking fragments of the window out of my trailing prayer shawl, naked in it but for cotton underwear. "Run!"

I flee down Harvard, up Greenwood, across Fowler, through the backyards of Erie Street. Where?

Fire engines are screaming everyplace. The flames pursue me. Pillars of smoke rage from Codman Square, Grove Hall, Talbot Ave., Morton. Everyone is pouring down wooden steps into the streets, nightgowns, undershirts, naked, a hail of rocks and laughter, laughter, everywhere.

"Franklin Park!"

Yet when I stumble through a maze of side streets up Esmond to the hill, the Avenue is a wall of rainbow, blue yellow, orange, exploding oil trucks, gas lines, its asphalt bed buckles and, crumbling with heat, showers of spark from the snapping electrical wires.

"Jump!"

Are you crazy? Look! I swing round only to see Esmond street in flame behind me. The golden shapes are hovering in the air, fanning destruction with their wings. A torch touches the seat of my pants and I jump into rainbow.

42

I can't even scream as I find myself springing forward on the cool green grass of Franklin Park, the fire behind me but a lump of live coal stuck into my mouth, lips seared, seething around the glowing bitumen, sunk into the soft edge of its tar, the brittle white enamel of my teeth. My flesh is burning, my tongue charred, yet I cannot spit it out and the ash is too hot for my fingers, a scalding hunk of Blue Hill Ave.

Woe is me, unclean. I am unclean. Asphalt seals my words. Where shall I flee?

"Who?" calls the chorus, their breath lighting the cinder in my mouth. "Who's chasing you?"

Rabbis, a whole academy of them, hoary beards are leaping in my wake, shaking their canes, young boys with silken earlocks and first fuzz clinging to their cheeks, brandishing the *Shulhan Arukh:* they sprint like hares from the bushes and grass of the Park, crying, "Maishe, Maishe!" to beat me to death.

An ancient in a high silk hat, striped pants, morning coat, rises on a gilt throne resting on a sledge carried on the shoulders of his fur-capped followers, directs the chase. He points to me, calling signals to his *shammus* who blows it out in code on a ram's horn. The Rabbis spread out in a net to flank my run.

What shall I do?

"Hide."

I somersault, flip, reverse myself, doubling back in my tracks, losing my charred shorts, top, naked in white shawl and black arm-straps. To the bleating of the *shofar*, I throw the Chassidim into confusion by cutting right across the throne of the grandee. Shout up . . .

Trayf! A rabbinical degree from a Pennsylvania bargain basement. Kosher hoodlum, I despise your sacrifices.

43

"Mamzer," he hooted. "You'll pay. Get him! *Kak im un!"*
The Boston English High School football team burst as
coursers from under his sledge, thundering after me with
oversized hams in blue-silk pants and shirts, "Break dat Jew
boy's head!" the captain calls, throwing himself at my heels
in a tackle. I skip away, leaving the team entangled with a
wing of B.U. Hillel toughs. I hasten toward the zoo.

Here are my friends. Have I not promised them peace, that
they will lie down together, wolf and lamb, lion and calf,
tickling and nuzzling each other: the kid licking at the leop-
ard's dugs.

Flinging open the heavy door to the house of the large
cats, I rush in. My feet make sticky sounds across the floor,
blood, slow, half lapping at my ankles, congealing. The tiger lies
slumped against the bars, butchered carcass, his fur stripped
off so only the blue flesh outlines a feline form against
the bones. I hear the tom-toms and the drums, Ashanti
chants and Pequod war whoops, smell the smoke of barbe-
cue. The warriors are returning for fresh meat. On I fly
through the back door, past the staved in coops of peacocks,
vultures, bald eagles, and the great horned owl. In the background I hear grinding of garbage trucks. The grandee has
bought off the Mayor. They lumber like tanks into the zoo
area, Rabbis sitting on their fenders, and I recognize among
them my teachers from elementary school, Miss McKenna,
Miss Riley, Miss MacNamara, Miss Maloney, sniffing the air
sharper than dogs.

I bolt. Oaks, elms, maples, into the woods; at the end of an
avenue of pines in a hidden corner of the Park is the rocky
brow of the old sage's farm, Canterbury, where he gamboled
as a boy with his brothers, hide and seek. Protect me, ghost.
The shriek of Miss McKenna of the sixth grade—hysterical,

44

unmarried, baying—sounds only a few yards away.

I jump. Blind, run without knowing where I am, deaf to the crackling of boughs, twigs snapping as I tear a way through the undergrowth on my knees among the leaves with snakes, my fingers groping in the holes of the basilisk, clambering up stone walls, across stuffed drainage ditches, rolling downhill, tumbling, head over heels, hide me, hide me, I beg, and with a crash, collide—my cheek against a tree.

I might be in my backyard, rubbing the craggy bark of the old oak tree. Massy, towering, its branches start forty feet above my head, the roots buckling up out of the grass. Holding it tight, my arms hugging a waist thick as a house, I creep around; the sweet sticky incense of cedar is in my nose and my fingers touch a crevice, crack in the wooden creature's side. A cave, I discover as I circle with my cheek pressed to its fragrant shingle, large enough to conceal me if I duck and stand up inside the trunk.

Not even the acutest nun can sniff me out in the deep waves of frankincense that wash from the veins of the cedar. The coal has fallen from my mouth. I listen to the Rabbis, gangs, garbage trucks, scampering in the Park, the sound of so many squirrels; and rejoice as they squeak, passing and repassing the tree.

I feel night come on, the light dying in the upper branches, darkening shadows at the roots, my prayer shawl glows white and milky in the circumference of the tree. Voices come near again, although now there is a strange hum, the swarming of wasps, hornets.

"O.K."

"Let 'er rip!"

I hear gruff accents through a wooden door, the hum a buzzing.

"Stickin' right out!"

"Just about here, Sir?"

"Wight! Wight! Just wight."

Teeth are scraping in the bark opposite my mouth, shaking back and forth, biting.

I look down and see that as the silver shawl spills to my feet, its fringes lie outside the tree. Wedged into the trunk, I try to yank them in.

"Wook, wook! It's awive!"

"Too late, buddy. This tree is sick."

The chain saw is chewing in the cedar and my teeth meet it, greedy, with a last kiss goodbye, Dorchester, tasting perfumed splinters, oil, metal, tooth, ash, and the forbidden mouthful of my own cup, blood.

Messages

I was searching through the telephone directory for Barbara among the Fratarollis, Fratatonnis, Frattacellis, Fratagionnis; four of them, one with three residences, Beacon Hill, a summer house in Marblehead, a downtown office, construction company; another with two, dentist and residence in Watertown. East Boston listed two, Rosie and Anthony. I dialed Rosie.

"Hello, Barbara there?"

"Bahbara? No, she's ovah her muddah's house. You tell her don' fahwget nex' Sunday, *o romperò il culo!*"

"Right."

"Sunday, Sunday, don' fahwget."

The digits leaped before my eyes to Anthony's. I was provided with a message for my errand. Hearts and arrows like a teen-age fool I stroked on the frost-bitten window of my telephone booth, the heavy tome of the Boston directory swinging back into place, the thud of my soul as the phone rang on a street in East Boston.

"Barbara?"

"Who is this?" The voice high and clipped. This could not be the sister of jovial Rosie, her wide heart that had already taken me into the family, a *paisana*, garlanding my brows, instructions thrust into my mouth.

"Maishe."

"Who?"

"Who is this?"

"This is Barbara's mother." I felt a cold wind off Massachusetts Bay shiver through the house in Eastie, formerly Noddles Isle. The hothouse warmth of my telephone booth, luxuriant blooms of my breath against the glass side, gaudy expectations, began to wilt. A moment before I had trodden the warm gardens of Neapolitan villas, crushing sun-baked pebbles; now Copley Square icicles came up between my toes. The raw stony heart of Boston whistled through the chill holes of the receiver. "Who is this?"

"A friend of Barbara's."

"What's your name?"

"Maishe."

"Maishe?"

"Maishe."

"Maishe what?"

I mumbled my last name, trying to roll the final syllable, spaghetti around the fork in my throat.

"You live around here?"

"No."

"Where do you live?"

"Dorchester."

"What part?"

"Warner Street."

A pause, "Where's that near?"

"Harvard Street, Blue Hill Ave."

"Oh . . ." skilled demographer and statistician, I could see the lines of Mrs. Frataronne's chart, race, religion, and relativity running down to zero. Boston geography. Did not my ancestors inhabit East Boston? Fifty years ago they were probably cooking in your kitchen; Mrs. Frataronne, let me come back to my old neighborhood. But Barbara's mother spoke to me now in a voice, hushed, personal, threatening, pronouncing my first name with the familiarity of cold, sticky pasta.

"Maishe, how old are you?"

I lopped off a decade, squeaking into the receiver, trying to force pimples and blemishes through the copper cable. Mrs. Frataronne, how wise age is, how desirous!

"Aren't you a little old for Barbara?"

"Well . . . ah . . . I . . ." stumbling, my mouth full of icy noodle, "No, ah . . . Barbara . . ." I steadied myself, a blizzard of mozzarella was blowing in the open door of the booth, "Barbara is very intelligent . . . for her age."

I brushed the powder stinging in my eyes, nose, from my face. "I . . . I'm a student."

"Where?"

Where should I admit myself, Wentworth Institute, Suffolk, Boston College, B.U., Emerson? Harvard or Tufts would scare her off. I scrambled through sheepskins in my glass cage, rolling, unrolling, looking for the mystical formula to lure East Boston mothers into beatitude. "I have a scholarship at Suffolk." True. It has been waiting for me fifteen years there, bright and shiny as the bronze goddess I was given as its token, a prize won for twisting myself into

49

grotesque shape, declaiming the hunchback king of Shakespeare. I had four years promised to me at that cubbyhole behind the State House as my classmates streamed off to Yale, Princeton, Stanford. Suffolk forbidden to me in my father's eyes as unclean meat.

Mrs. Frataronne cleared her throat for a moment, puzzled, my demi-truth scrambling her intricate diagram.

"What year are you in?"

My tongue flabby, overripe, full of holes, stuttered out the words, best I could make of my predicament, "I'm right now on leave."

"What do you do?"

"Read. I'm reading, catching up . . ." It was too late. Mrs. Frataronne sliced into my tongue.

"Maishe. I think Barbara should see boys of her own age and background."

That was it. Clean as the click of the receiver on the other end. I, holding two black balls in my hand at either end of a stiff plastic rod. I try to turn. The telephone box is crammed with trash. Tissue paper, balls rolled up by watery-eyed, runny-nosed Bostonians. Boles and boles of it have blown into the booth. Crushed into a glass coffin with me, the paper hankies of the whole downtown blot, blot my tears.

The Cave

"Radishevtsky," I said, "show me the cave."

"Ooooh," he crooned. "What's the boy talking about?" sticking the bone of his nose into yellow fluff, tickling it in beaten egg whites, custard blossoms on his nostril warts.

"Please?" I asked. "I know you know."

"Holes, Maishe. I know holes. You want to cross Boston from Forest Hills, go down in greenery at the Arboretum and come out in the salt marsh, Columbia Point or Savin Hill, I'll help. Sewer lines, tunnels, the secret passageway between the State House and City Hall that runs through the First National Bank vault? Everyone knows it. Caves, what caves?"

"Radishevtsky?"

"Maishe, you think I'm a mystic all of a sudden? I'm a pessimist, a rationalist. Let Barbara Frataronne show you a cave, hah."

I stuck my finger in his custard bowl. "Nasty boy," he

chuckled. "Suck!"

Turning around in the Bickford, I started out.

"Stop!" he shouted, still looking into his pudding.

"You're a fake," I screamed.

"Who's pretending?" he mocked, staring into the round clay pot.

"You drove her away. For what? Dirty jokes? Dried leaves? Making fun of a crazy priest? Show me the other world, Radishevtsky, or lose your last disciple."

"I see trouble," he intoned, "a dead snake, seven dried oak leaves and a stale cornbeef sandwich."

"*Narishkeyt!*" I rushed back in and knocked the white custard bowl off his table, spinning, shattering on the floor.

"Hey! Hey!" The white-jacketed zombies behind the counter come to life, scenting broken crockery; the short-order cooks, red with steam plunging from the kitchen, all graduates of Mass. Psychopathic, hallooing, "Hey! Hey!"

"Save me," he whispers. I scoop him up into my arms. Nothing. He weighs nothing. I hold a sack full of feathers.

"Radishevtsky?"

"Quick," he says, "The cave."

I run with my bundle of quills out the door of the Bickford, a pack of howling white-coated maniacs crowding through the plate glass behind me, brandishing knives, forks, spoons. "Hippies, kikes, bums!" We flee with them at our coattails, dodging traffic; rush into the Greyhound Terminal, the bus to Bangor, Maine, calling, "Emergency! Emergency!" run down the aisle to the Emergency Exit and yanking it open, jump out while the bus driver is entangled at the entrance with our boarding party.

"Copley Square," in my ear.

The buses are giving chase. Great silver hearses slide out of

52

the concrete crib, engines growling, dozens of buses speeding toward us, a glut of shining chrome carriage converging on me, radioing to their compatriots at Trailways and the M.T.A. Headlights on, they roll to pin us against the walls of the Parking Garage, Trinity Church, when Radishevtsky arises in my arms, spreading his black sackcloth and we soar above the back fire of exhaust pipes, beyond the Custom House tower, John Hancock, Prudential, so far we can see Trimountaine, the old three-cornered hill gleaming as the retreating ice cap tears away the rubble of brick and concrete, unstoppers the dikes, lets the Charles waves flood over Back Bay, Commonwealth Ave., the brine of the Atlantic creeping up the mountain's flanks, flinging away the iron beams of the expressway, floating them off to Labrador. Ponds seep up out of the gutters and sewage systems, broken mains, sweet springs, grasses take root again, the hill tops red with strawberries, raspberries bramble, blueberry bush, flocks of duck, wild pigeon, sea gull, owl, eagle; schools of herring are teeming in the inner harbor, rubbing their scales silvery against the gut of Indian weirs stretched across the cove where the Boylston Street Subway stood, shoals of cod, mackerel, bass, haddock, perch, bushels of shiner, pollack; gamboling against the shores, a sea alight with fish. Wolves, packs of them, sniffing the new marsh salts oozing in the Bay, are running, snapping at the haunches of the bear who shambled forward to the feast, foxes, deer, the trumpet of the moose, all tumbling pell-mell to Trimountaine.

See, as we soar, the sun scudding off into the horizon, a salmon-ribbed sky sailing by the green hollow bowl of land, puffed by a clean breeze off the Atlantic and there it gleams, one white patch, a sickly square of canvas on whose piles swarm pale germs, eager to infest.

53

We dive. Descend in the darkness of early morning to a Copley Square deserted, free of cars, pedestrians, police, on the lawn of the grass triangle before Trinity Church, fog shrouding the gargoyles on its battlements.

"Dig," barks Radishevtsky. He pulls out the silver spoon from his custard bowl, drawing it from a deep pocket of his black shroud.

I force its lip through the crust of moist, thin grass, pebbles, cigarette butt, crumbling match stick, touch the black loam, scoop and throw it over my shoulder.

"Dig!"

I strike rubble, the brick wall of an old country lane, mussel shells, sink feet through marsh mud, throwing up fish heads, then the first bright knobs of copper, a silver seam, at last the shovel rises gilt with yellow.

"Radishevtsky," I weep, "Master!" But looking up I see that it is not the moon shining in, illuminating my efforts but the brilliant ceiling of the vault. The light is coming from the metal I am working through. Spoonfuls cling to the roof over my head. The gravedigger has sealed the shaft above.

I throw the spoon on the pitted floor of my chamber, ready to die in the golden bubble.

Breathing my own oxygen, betrayed into a crypt. I scratch with my fingers at the splendid bottom of the tomb among the soft metal of the nuggets, throwing the dust on my head, the flame in me guttering, my eye waxing old.

"Dig."

The voice is below me, shrill and metallic in the echo of the bubble. My thumb pokes in its direction and breaks through into a hole. I put my fist through, then my arm, butt with my head, and, squeezing forward, open my eyes in a tunnel.

I take deep breaths of soft, wet air.

"Maishe, hurry up. The club is meeting."

A tiny man, a peanut, four feet high with a sallow yellow face, wisps of grey hair and ragged orange teeth is smiling up at me. He wears a faded three-piece suit.

It's the scholar. I know him from his walks through Harvard Square on the way to The Old Howard or the movies. In the wide brow sitting on that short stump, the whole history of philosophy is catalogued A to Z in a dozen languages, Greek, Church Latin, Hebrew, Arabic, Sanscrit, all hand-scribbled in commentary on white paper with wide blue margins, footnotes as dense as the constellations swarming through the great stars, Plato, Philo, Aristotle, Augustine, Spinoza. He put his face up next to mine so that I could smell the breath, musty, stale with the decay of old pages, the real odor of sanctity. His eyes sparkled and he pinched my cheek.

"Be careful," he whispered.

"Of what?"

"In public . . ."

"But . . ."

"Between you and me," he laughed, a dry peppery chuckle like a naked pen point jabbing an overblown argument. He wiped his tongue in the corner of his lip, "Say anything."

He put out a frail hand to steady me as I pushed out of the bubble to join him in the long tunnel where he stood. Winking, as I jumped to my feet beside him. "Only write it in Hebrew."

He took my hand in his delicate stubby fingers, lined and crossed with all the wrinkles in philosophy. "Tonight there are a lot of *goyiim*." Turning, we trekked down the tunnel together, deep into the bowels of Boston.

At length we came to an enormous underground room.

"This is the cave," I exclaimed.

"A facsimile," he corrected, "And of course there are more caves than one. You remember the crevice in which Simeon Ben Yohai and his son Eleazar were concealed for thirteen years? The pit where King David watched a spider weave? And Machpelah? However, take a seat." He motioned me to a rickety wooden bench. "We'll sit here."

Across the way was a polished marble couch between two slim Ionic colonnades; farther along, the elaborate scrollwork of Byzantine and Roman furniture, Arab cushions brightly banded scattered here and there. The only adornment of our corner was a cardboard box full of books. "Fancy, eh," he whistled, watching my stare.

"In your honor," he said, pursing his lips with sly pleasure, "You can pick the topic."

"Topic?"

"Ask a question."

I looked at the kindly old man and his face, the blood blotted in ink spots across the massive forehead. His cheeks glowed, eerie and dark. I felt so foolish and insignificant, a flunk out, class booby, sitting in the bottom row of my Hebrew School, dreaming out the window, the tears damp on my chin, panic tearing in my chest at the teacher's voice, wanting to throw myself out into the yard below. Unto me, I bit my tongue, confusion of face.

"Ask."

I floundered, wringing my hands, shaking. They would throw me out. I could think of nothing as my self-disgust hurled me down and I blurted out only to fling foolishness in his face:

"My mother, where is she?"

The hole burst into fire. White light, sheets of it, shattered about me.

"Ah!" I felt his hand touch my cheek like the thumbing of a page. "A good boy."

I looked up into his bright eyes. "An old favorite."

The room was filled with people, a crowd of ancients, draped in sheets, shawls, short skirts. My friend called out, "Aetius! Where's his mother?"

"The stars are animals."

"Interesting," my teacher whispered. "He thinks he's quoting Aristotle. Not clear of course. A strange tack but perhaps we'll find her."

"Is she a star?"

"Maybe. What do you think?"

"What good is it?"

He pointed his finger at an elderly man in the room. "According to Simplicius here, she would, could, hear you, see you, and touch you."

"Wonderful," I cried.

"However, she could not taste you or smell you."

What kind of ghost would I hold in my arms? I remember the taste of her mouth as she kissed me so hard my lip was bitten, dying, the smell of the sweat on her upper lip as I hugged her swollen body to me.

"According to Saint Thomas quoting Alexander she would be a 'living being' only in 'an equivocal sense'—that is, she would not be possessed of a 'nutritive power'."

"Are you crazy?" I cried. "I grew in her, a vegetable, a lump of flesh, I swelled in her tummy."

"Maishe, please," said a handsome but nervous young man. "If you want your mother to be a star, her soul must be pure and a philosophic one. Taste, smell, these are disgusting attributes; distracting when we are thinking of eternity. If you want your mother to be a beet, a potato, fine."

A seedy looking Arab sidled up to me, muttering in my ear. "Don't let him get away with that *mishiguss*. According to him, she doesn't even have imagination."

"No imagination?"

"What does she need it for? She's probably an angel, spinning, moved by divine desire, will. She has appetence."

"Appetite," shouted the Arab. "Let her have an appetite instead."

Laughter through the room. Aetius shouted over the din, "The stars are animals."

"She's not a star," I said to my friend. The laughter continued. I noticed now in the center of the discussion a long wooden box, about three feet wide and six feet long. Polished boards stained dark, gleaming with varnish, and adorned only with a simple star of two intersecting triangles. It was from this crate that the laughter resounded in a hollow booming echo.

"Well let's think of something else," the scholar replied. "There are several Stoics here who could give you back your mother."

"Yes!"

"The question is where? This doctrine of *palingenesis* holds that there are worlds before and worlds to come that are the exact duplicate of the world we are in now. Your mother would receive a resurrection, letter perfect. However . . ."

"However what?"

"You have to give up your belief in 'eternal life'. This is only an endless series of comings back to the same 'temporary life'. Moreover, as Tatian says, 'for no useful

58

purpose'."

Bewildered, I shook my head. The stoics smiled at me, impassive.

"You can have her back right now," a short man in a bed sheet whistled, "No tricks."

"That was Pythagoras," my friend remarked, "A little out of date."

"Can't we do business?"

"If you want her as a plant, a vegetable, or residing in another body, fine. His theory is transmigration of the soul. But there is no assurance she won't have jumped into a cat."

Pythagorus hissed and made mewing sounds. "Not so bad, eh?" he encouraged.

"No," I turned away. "I don't want it."

"Maybe we should talk to the Church Fathers."

"Is that kosher?"

"Maishe, you have to be broad-minded. Frankly, we're all working on the same ideas. Give a little, take a little, what's the difference? Believe me, they owe us plenty. Don't be ashamed to ask a bit in return. Was your mother wicked?"

"My mother?"

"For the sake of argument. Keep cool. We don't even talk then to Arnobius, a minor point of view, actually, that wicked souls are annihilated."

"Annihilated?"

"Let's start with a solid axiom. You think that your mother's still around?"

"Please, please." I was crying.

"If you just want her to be around, that's enough. Immortality, resurrection . . ." he sang to a show tune, "You can't have one . . . without the ah . . . ah . . . ah . . . aaahther!

"O.K. Cheered up?"

"Yes," I sniffed.

"The question is what will she look like? Origen, who doesn't buy this annihilation business, anyway, says that you will find her with a spiritual body."

"What's that mean?"

"Your mother would retain an individual form as a spiritual being identical with her animal being but not necessarily the same figure or shape. This is based on a common germ, or spermatic logic.

"Is this the fellow who cut off his balls?"

"According to a modern commentary, however, 'his spiritual testicles remained'."

"I don't trust him."

"Neither do the other Church Fathers. They want a more literal body in the hereafter. 'Auto Tooto!' says Gregory of Nyssa, 100 percent the same. Iraneus is giving the same guarantee—for eternity. Tertullian offers 'absolute integrity' of mouth, throat, teeth, belly, and bowels, and throwing in an assurance of separate sex parts, phallus and pudenda. Augustine at the end of the strip sets his seal on a deal with no finagling, those who get up for the resurrection 'will be bodies and not spirits . . . As far as regards substance, even then it shall be flesh.' "

"Hooray!" I cried.

The saints were beaming at me.

"Of course, there are questions. What's the good of the body, if the body is immortal?"

"I don't understand."

"Well, every organ of the body has a special use. In heaven, however, where there is no necessity, what use will the organs of the body have?"

My head shook in my hands. It was too complicated.

"Listen," said my friend. "Talking of bodies, if this is boring, we could take off and go to the burlesque. There's a terrific show at the Apollo tonight. Candy Apple and Rue La Rue.

"Presto," he called out. Stage curtains parted in the midst of the columns and benches. A line of beautiful girls came out kicking to the sound of cymbals and trap drums, a wheezing saxophone.

> Oh they don't wear pants
> In the sunny part of France
> Bam bam, ba ba ba bam bam . . .

It was the Pony Ballet of The National Council of Jewish Women, Junior Division, Bridgeport, Conn. My mother threw out her long lovely legs in short pants and a sailor blouse. "Ma!" I cried, but it faded in an instant.

"Where is she?" I shook the scholar's arm.

"All right," he sighed, nodding his head sleepily, "back to business. I knew it couldn't last. We wouldn't find her there according to anyone. The Epicureans claim she'll be enjoying 'static pleasure'. It's always something high falutin' like that: 'the highest and surest joy' or 'freedom from mental disturbance . . . impassible flesh . . .' and a lot of other Novocain."

"Why?"

"You want her to suffer after death?"

"No," I answered without thinking. "I don't think so."

"Why should she suffer?"

"No reason," I stammered. "She was a saint. She suffered believe me, more than her share."

"Why?"

"Me," I wept. "I made her suffer."

"All right, she won't suffer."

61

"How will she know me though, if her flesh is impassive?"

The laugh started from the box again, deep and racking, shaking my bones.

"She's in there!" I screamed. "I know that voice! It's her. It's her. Help me, master, help me!"

"Will you take her, free from 'sorrow and sighing', from 'bodily pain and affliction of soul'?"

"Anyway, I'll take her," I exclaimed. "Animal, vegetable, mineral, spirit or body! Blind, deaf, dumb, just let me touch her again. Please, please I'll do anything."

"Irenaeus," he called, "Gregory, Tertullian, Lactantius, hurry, give us a hand with the lid. The Fathers rushed forward, tears of joy running down their cheeks, congratulating me. They stuck their huge iron crosses like crowbars under the lid of the box to jimmy it open. It creaked and gave way, rising when a voice rang out above.

"Get away from dat coffin."

The scholar groaned, "I was afraid. Afraid."

"Get away from it boys. It stinks."

The voice harsh, hoarse, unmistakable Boston Irish. "She's goin' to Hell and you *know* it."

"Who is this?" I demanded.

The early Fathers, their faces beet red, slunk back from the box.

"Yah mudduh stinks."

I look up where the voice is coming from. It echoes down a long tapering fly space over the stage where the Pony Ballet had danced. At the very apex I see a red dot shouting into this uncanny natural bullhorn.

"Watch your mouth," I call up.

"Yah know whay-uh yah kikes ahr goin'?"

I shook my fist.

"Tell 'em Augie!"

St. Augustine squirmed in a corner of the cave, his black cheeks glowing like brick with shame, looking down at his sandals, afraid to face the scholar and me, "Man, I do regret this, like . . ."

"He used to be a Manichaean, you know everything was black and white, good and evil . . ." interposed my guide trying to extenuate his friend.

"All yah pals know what dah score is, Iky. C'mon Clem, tell'm whay-uh his mudduh is!"

The Alexandrian shifted his eyes from us, mumbling in Greek.

The red dot cloven into two lips let out a shaky thunderclap with a laughing cloud of stinking gas. "Dat's dah dogma foh yah Yiddles."

The stench of hereafter from Boston Baked Beans exploded in the cave, lurid orange puffs, foul and noxious. Catcalls from the shattered philosophers coughing raspberries, vulgarisms, "Go back to B.C., Father!"

"Are you B.C. or A.C.?"

"Didn't I see you in Dover Street?" We were thrown upward in a swirling cone, a fiery tempest corkscrewing to the top of the hole.

"Grab the coffin," called the little man as he floated away.

I reached for my mother's casement as it whirled to the top, a wooden torpedo, sucked after, tumbled into the open air, came down through green branches of elm trees, twigs and leaves breaking my fall from the heavens into the midst of octogenarians, drunks, prostitutes, college students, high-school kids, a sprinkling in tweeds, dresses and suits, all shouting at once at a short silver-haired priest, carmine-cheeked.

"Hayyl May-ree," he howled back.

"Hayyl yourself."

"Hayyl Hitler!" barked another.

"We all know," he screeched, "That awll jewwws mah-stah-bate in bed."

Whistles and popping noises.

"Will evewy Jewww who mah-stahbates in bed, put his hand above his head?"

"Father, look!"

All heads turn deep into the center of the mob where the voice came from. I recognize it. "You've got *your* hand in the air."

The priest's palm slinks down slowly, clutching the crucifix. He murmurs, putting lips to it: "Annihilate, annihilate . . ."

I push my way through the mob to Radishevtsky but he is weeping, large colorless drops oozing in pear-shaped globules. "You too," he caws but breaks down in tears.

The priest ignores him, intent on his cross.

The Brandeis students are singing "Kol Nidre". The drunks "Auld Lang Syne". Radishevtsky is on his knees, "Grass, all grass. And even the grass." It is crushing us all into nothing, even the heretic Father looking up, feels the might of it, the pull from the hole where all worlds will be extinguished.

"May-ree," whimpers the priest. "Mayree."

"Full of sh . . ." I cry when the rod strikes me. A skinny black umbrella, tightly furled, whacking at my head in short, determined chops. A dignified, thin-lipped lady dressed in dark mourning weed wields it, knocking. Her white hair neatly gathered in a bun, blue cheeks primly drawn in, she brings down the steel shank of the ruler as hard as she can in one final, elementary correction.

Hub

It took a while to find the path. There are roads to take you to Providence, New York, Springfield, Chicago, or even, God speed, with a few ferries, Jerusalem or Peking: fine black asphalt with three or four lanes running in either direction doing amazing loops and clover leafs within the intersections. Our city is called The Hub and there are still spokes in the downtown with cobbles underfoot, country lanes, macadam, tar, dirt. I could have had my pick, marching out of Boston, only a *taliss* bag and the wine-red binding of Schlossberg's Funeral Chapel prayer book for company—and with all the road maps in the world, Sunoco, Mobil, Gulf, the winged horse, the golden conch, a flying Aleph—still not have stumbled on the site.

No, someone put me on the right path. Stumbling last night into a side street, starting to trace my way in triangles, octagons, combining parallelogram and a complicated rhombus, I picked up the track—a flight of fat gray pigeons on my left, a convoy of aerial battleship ringed with a gaudy flash of peacock rainbow at the neck, city birds guided me far out into the hills and highland beyond Trimountaine.

Not the metropolis's history that I am treading back in now, only my own, 22 years, you can work magic circling. I pass the hateful industrial brick of the Boston Public Latin School, the green lawns of the Sarah Greenwood Elementary, find myself in the dim corridors of my Hebrew academy, the Beth El, out in the back alley threading a way between huge steel garbage cans. Now I am in a large pantry at the Hecht House and I can hear the other kids in the nursery crying for milk and cookies as I push out the back door on my way, through yards littered with coal ash, wet cardboard, tin cans, broken bottles, along a collapsed picket fence, squeezing through iron railings into a strange park of wide lawns, old trees, adults in pajamas strolling through, smiling at me, giggling.

"Want to play? Play?" they ask as I walk away slipping through twisted black rods again, finding at the bottom of a ravine between the rusting bodies of ancient automobiles, a tiny stream mottled in emerald algae, my Sambatyon, flowing from Eden.

My tiny legs are tired and I have wet my pants but I wade in, cross, hold my white sox and brown oxfords in my free hand, hoping I will meet someone who can tie my shoes.

The pigeons sway about my head and I turn my pocket out, scattering the last sugar crumbs of a cookie someone put in my pocket.

There is such a sweet smell coming from the blue velvet bag in which my small prayer shawl lies and a single square of silk black *yarmulke* that I open it up and discover springs of

66

blossom, pear and apple, cherry too, white and pink flags of the fruit flesh, so now I know that my wallet has been stuffed for the journey. The birds are twittering. Did I pass through my old backyard in the night, breaking them off? The pigeons pluck up these thoughts, cooing and clucking, gorging themselves on the last crumbs of sadness, chasing off the past, flapping at my elbows. I put the black skullcap on my head. The child's white-silk prayer shawl around my shoulders, its gold collar sparkling in the sun, and close the blue bag full of honey blossoms.

I wave goodbye to the birds who turn back, wheeling in the sky, to Boston.

I set my shoes, scuffed brown toes, trailing strings, gossamer threads of the shawl fringes, in the faint path along the river bank and stepping softly over the new grasses, dandelion green, orange crown, wood violet, grape iris: smelling the mint in the clefts of the rock along the water, following its sinuous winding flowing before me, past me, behind me as the stream doubles upon itself, dips from its tributaries to one channel of the Bay, then the other, Charles, Neponset. My feet sink down into the marsh mud, the dark puddle rising above my ankles, knees, waist; the blue bag in my hand floats above the ripples, puffing, buoyant. I clamber onto its springing center, the pear and apple boughs ribbing the velvet boat. Swiftly we drift in an eddy of the current, around and around, in a flat, watery plain, muskrats paddling up beside us as we thread our way through this New England Sargossa of cattail, skunk cabbage, submerged blue grasses. A spring breeze full of flowers struck our craft aft and we sailed south, all of a sudden, against the current, river banks opening before us, upstream.

I catch the wind in my skullcap.

"Maisheh," calls a voice in the rush of breath that puffs our barque and bears it aloft over the waters.

"What?" I ask, straining to hold on to the black *yarmulke* brimming so it threatens to fly out of my hands or tip us over.

"Maisheh," I hear again, standing on my tiptoes, holding on to my velvet boat by a few yellow strands of its gold embroidery, lashing them around the fingers of my hand so as not to blow away.

"Here I am."

All around me it calls, my name warm and soft in its utterance. "Maisheh, Maisheh," filled with the sound of lost uncles, aunts, grandpas, and hers, calling, "Maisheh, Maisheh."

"What?"

"Tie your shoes."

"I can't"

"Try."

I withdraw my fingers from the golden cords which hold the *yarmulke* puffed out. I stoop to my untied shoes, the sturdy brown strings, limp to the left and right.

"Cross them," she instructs. I draw the right to the left, the left over the right. "Put your forefinger in the middle." I press down hard as I can, intent on getting it right. Hooking the loop with my thumb, inserting the strings into one another and like magic, firmly drawing it closed; a bow like a flower blossoms on my shoe and I feel the cord in my tummy catch, tugging me, my boat, into another . . . .

And it came to pass that we touched on a shore lit with lilies, long tapering trumpets, blowing creamy notes of perfume as we slowly rustled to rest within their midst. Behind us the breeze ceased in the white birches, slim bodies that had waved as we swept through their columns of snowy marble, a gate of shuddering woods.

Now all was still. Above me the hill, not the great blue one far off in the horizon, but a gentle half-hidden slope. Dreamy with lilies I drew my blue *taliss* bag out of the water. It shrank, the air seeping out of its belly, still dripping, the size of a baby blanket now. Inside, unzipping it, were the fruit boughs and my prayer book, dry. Taking the apple and pear in hand I started up.

Stepping on fragile petals, tiny violets of the field with only a watery tint of color yet so thick—a purple runner of them twisted with green shag under my feet.

Before I came over the top to look down, the scent of it rose to me so that my eyes misted with crystals of sugar, lemon and orange, lime and pomegranite. The oil of them going up from the branches, the sap on fire, smoking as I put my right foot down, then my left, my right in a speckled brown lady's slipper, then my left as I climbed over the crest.

Yes I knew it. I had seen it before. There was the pool of still waters. The lattice fronds of weeping willows, pink magnolias in flower, red dogwood, long white bridal veils stretched through whole fields of trees draped for a wedding. And, among the New England arbor, others, wide leafy terebinths, tamarisk, date palms, silver figs, and spreading its light through the very earth where its roots entangled with each of its children, that shining husk at the center from which our first parents were bidden, *essen, essen, mein kinder*, and which gleams still awaiting their return. *Ayl mole rachamem*, O God full of mercy.

I wander among the rectangular bronze tables, searching for my name. Here we left her by the edge of the waters under willows. On the brazen markers were hammered the names we had left behind forever. Marcus, Shore, Dreizen, Rosen, Sohmer, Epstein, all our neighbors from the old streets fled now to the three hundred and ten worlds assigned to each of the righteous, leaving behind the garb of patronyms and bones they had assumed in the exile.

Grass, the green grass, thick and matted, I see suddenly, my shoes stepping with fear over the fresh-cropped blades, the letters inscribing her portal. The name is as palpable as her body for which it stands and drawn toward the metal plate I float across the lawn feeling her grave and understanding eyes upon me, come to meet mine, judge, approve, disapprove, standing over her bed with my shoelaces tied, I say the prayers that were taught to me.

The pear and apple boughs about us as a bower. I have brought a pillow and a silken blanket. I will depart no more. Mamma, I whisper, stopping down to rest my head. Reach out and touch the letters.

A warm flush from her breast comes to my fingers. I lay my cheek against the door of bronze.

Onan's Child

One

And it came to pass at that time that Judah went down from his bretheren, and turned in to a certain Adullamite, whose name was Hirah. And Judah saw there a daughter of a certain Canaanite whose name was Shua, and he took her, and went in unto her. And she conceived and bore a son; and he called his name Er. And she conceived again, and bore a son; and she called his name Onan. And she yet again bore a son, and called his name Shelah; and he was at Chezib, when she bore him.

Genesis 38: 1-5

In the days of Manasseh, who adopted from his environment every remnant of star-worship and magic in Israel . . .

Martin Buber

My ancestor was Ham, dark-clouded Ham, father of Canaan, grandfather of Nimrod, Abraham's uncle, the sick son and the bearer of sin. A servant of that burden and often in the night I have felt in my great black organ as it lifts up, the golden sparklers of Babylon, stars erupting in my cursed, blessed *shtoupper*, the seed of all those lost cousins, Noah's generation, the men before the Flood.

Yes, I, Onan, alone of Jacob's loins, worshipped my fantastic ancestors and tried to sink into the fatal heat of their dreams, the warm earth that they sunk into, toes and ankles, knees pressing down into the sweet chocolate dough while they held the moon green and golden like a ripe and running cheese in their hands dipping nose and lips into the scum of creation.

Do not imagine that I am black, white, yellow, or red, though, no I am all the colors of the rainbow, that bough which unbends in my head, rising out of those turgid waters, dazed, purified ribbon which bound us back to the thick and steaming earth; they spoke still of that day when everything was cowled like a new-born baby, moist and damp, and the tender promises of seed were made.

I laughed. Dust cracked the old man's lips as he spoke, senile old fornicator, good to teach the babies tales, dreams of water, staked out as we were in a dry gulch, wetting our lips at the canteen mouth, his own stinking of wine, trying to make us memorize the genealogies. Still, I lingered in the tent.

I was dark then, brown as the spicy bark of the cinnamon, like all of Jacob's progeny, sun-baked, not blanched to the fatal white that wasted through my skin as the long afternoons under the rank hair of goatskins enclosed me in chapters of the secrets I had learned.

74

Too long among the babies. Er, my brother, the elder of us three, was long since out with uncles, horsing around sheep, annoying the camels, racing donkeys up and down the sand flats, tickling our girls after dark at the water hole, and long after even Shelah, my younger had toddled away, bored by the recitation, to shout and shoot his arrows, toy barbs, at the leather buttocks of our grandmothers, Leah, Bilhah, Zilpah, I lay among the cushions, half asleep, ashamed to be there, in the shadows, to hear him construct the fragile bones of gopher wood, bending the joints into a feathery ark which lifted under the slow swell below.

Jacob, Jacob, my blind grandfather who saw everything, the trickster tricked. Rape, thievery, adultery, murder, all the baggage that you piled into the family closet after those two old holies, Isaac and Abraham. And were you not a child of Canaan too, playing games with your father, did you not violate his nakedness?

Just as foolish, eyeless, as Isaac thought, that night, O sightless lust, you crawled on top of grandmother, fingering her tits thinking you were in the younger sister's thighs.

Your magic was meant for Rachel, Leah's ass too prosaic. It was Joseph my baby uncle you held by the wrist when the others filed from your bed out to the open air, bright sunlight, lowing of the herds, playtime! Joseph to whom you whispered the other stories and uncovered the miracle.

Did you see me out of the gloom, looking through the space under the tent pegs; knowing, helpless to shade me from the mystery I was too weak to bear.

Madness.

Joseph found that out, his mouth opening up and driving brothers, step-mothers, you too, his father, crazy.

Now even as I waste into death, the coarse shadow of the

75

woman in the corner here haunting me to the end, breasts that for all their beauty as she sweeps by in her robes, sag foolishly if you stare without passion in the brutal light of morning, her calves misshapen when she has loosed them from her sandals, even the arch of her behind lower than it should be, the whole of her sad, a lump of flesh, dying even as I die myself, I see that gleaming bone, inhuman spot, Jacob drawing his skirts up in the lightless tent, the toes, ankle, kneecap, no different than any old man's but lit up, glowing, and I knew now what the tale he had told of Ham meant, why my ancestor had crept in on his father lying drunken, ecstatic, probing the female nature of the Unknowable, am I not Noah's son too, only it was old man's work, not for the young to see and you fell speechless dumb and the burden of it—a slave now, your head downcast from the light, not what you thought was there, upright that fountain from which you burst but a nakedness, an unveiling—shame! struck him down and now as the brilliant shank where the angel's finger had twisted my grandfather's loin was uncovered I shrank back, the glut of it in my throat, leaving two of them, grandfather and baby uncle, too young, too old, to be hurt—bathed in white heat, the miracle.

Two

And Judah took a wife for Er, his first born, and her name was Tamar. And Er, Judah's first born, was wicked in the sight of the Lord: and the Lord slew him. And Judah said unto Onan: 'Go unto thy brother's wife and perform the duty of a husband's brother unto her, and raise up seed to thy brother.'

Genesis 38— 6-8

She is stirring again in the corner. Moving the cushions restlessly. I can taste the sweat under the dark fuzz of her upper lip and smell even here at the opposite end of the tent that scent perfume and heat boiling under armpits, between her legs, filling this home.

Last night she came at me, rose suddenly as the sun died in the tent flaps, unveiling and letting me see the underclothes dropping from her haunches, drawing the dress up swiftly over her head and standing in the murky gold of the lamps she lit for the spectacle a moment before, she swayed, laughing, letting the heavy olive tits swing away from her chest, shaking the curves of her buttock as she strutted, parading, even banging the tambourine she flashed suddenly, sleight of hand, thumping it upon her private parts smiling all the while, slyly, showing me two perfect rows of white teeth.

I had to break and run, the doorway—it was there it happened, she lunged deep into my robes, gripped me by it, screeching, knowing she had me, stiff and furious, that I could not help myself, had been lying, as she suspected, anything but impotent. I had to push, claw, beat her off like a beast before I could get out into the camp and the cold desert night.

Brazen, mocking, shameless, yet she did not follow, knowing her limit, the tent space: and avoiding my father, uncles, I stepped by side paths outside the circle of dogs, watchmen, into the wilderness.

I was still stiff. Under the cotton cloths on my loins the member was stuck packed with stars.

And above my head they pricked. Spangles pressing my flesh, each one tickling me until I leapt, trying to draw myself up on their fiery straight strings. I stretched on the taut lines of their dissection, a whole universe of sharp wires running through my body.

And fumbling with my fingers, I tried to push myself up to this harp, send the music shuddering through all, my joy darting from the gut, in flight, flight.

Penetrated.

Yes, here I could imagine her ass, perfect round plump, sun-ripened peach splitting a hot orange pulp apart, its juice wet against the mouth, fuzz tickling the upper lip as you sank into it relishing even the bitter taste of the pit.

And my brother, scar at the edge of his lip where the knife had caught him cutting the sneer into his face, snapping the girdle apart, stripping away the soft wrappings, biting into the fat of her arms and cheeks until she screamed in horror, brutalizing her anus with his thumb and cock until the tears sent such a flash through him he did not dare to defy but drove himself, scraping and cursing, into the moist clinging center, his fingers knotting the black tresses below him, twisting them as she cried and tried to wrestle the beast now dying in her, sighing as they flowed away.

The sand prickled at the back of my neck. A coat of harsh orange beads, each sharp as a diamond scratched their blades across my flesh. My robes discarded beside me, the moon's white milk skimmed in the red bush of my crotch. I heard the wind come up and desolate I howled, finding myself congealed again into a lump of skin and gristle, no more than this, dream of dirt. And yet I had been warned, my grandmother raking my linen knew and shook her head at me, divining what would happen, clean life, clean heart, clean bed. She wanted no magicians in the family. Leave that to Rachel. One trick she had played, enough. She laughed at Joseph and his coat. "Please," she said. "Anyone else going around like that? A joke?" Her sons couldn't see it. Covetous, saw all the colors of the covenant shimmering. Noah's rainbow, Leah wouldn't weave for them. "Please, one is enough."

"One what?" my uncles, father, stormed. "One king?"

"Please, boys," she said. "He looks—a king?"

79

"A king," they shouted and ran out before she could get under their skins. No, I knew. He didn't look like any king in it and what he was, she didn't want for hers, any of her brood; that was Rachel's basket, my great aunt who stole her father's golden gods, a temptress good at spells, jinxing her own vagina. Leah had a laugh at Jacob, even his shining bone. "So he changed his name. He limps. He aged a bit. The best thing about it was he don't run around so much." She missed her sister, Rachel, "full of hocus-pocus but a lot of fun." Guilty about the swap but used to smile in the middle of the story. "Look," she'd sigh, "we were both Laban's daughters. Jacob had been half as bright as his ma, he would have known." And she doted on the dead one's baby. "No funny business with this Bennie. No bad dreams, fancy clothes, nothing. This one—going to be a good, sensible *boitchik*. Just like Auntie."

The day she found my linen, caught me by the wrist. "Who taught you this?" squeezing my funny bone, pushing me back against the tent pole. Then she let me go. Gave me a long dark look, shaking her head. "*Boitchik*, trouble, trouble, trouble!"

Now naked on the side of the dune, looking up into the cold glittering night I coveted Joseph's coat, Jacob's shining twisted sinew. Those red, green, blue, purple stripes that had suddenly dazzled the brothers one day Jacob's gift, threads that Leah knew no fingers in the camp could touch much less twist or cut and sew to shape so that my father's and uncles' murmurings were no better than the dumb grunts of Babel everyone gathered to push up a tower into the Heavens thinking brick by brick to climb into the heights of before and hereafter. Ha! Ha! My grandmother gave me a dirty look when I smirked at my father, complaining to us. If her son was a little thick that was fine. She was breeding for the future and hard knocks coming, nervous intelligence was showy goods not made to last. She didn't even bother to go out and look but just covered Benjamin's cradle, "He shouldn't get ideas."

Yet I stared when all the others saw were colors dancing off his body, the look in his eyes, a boy not older than myself swept up, walking not here on the packed earth of the camp but along the span of the covenant, his sandals sinking into fiery gold, green, red of the rim far away from us all as he made his way into the sky.

I stood there at the door of mist as the rainbow disappeared and Joseph standing like a statue here, stone cold, slowly came back to us; my uncles, color blind, seeing only he was indifferent to them, peacock proud, they whispered, tried to complain but Jacob could not understand. Blood was their hue, on their hands, the whole lot tainted, a hairy bunch of men crowding into his tent, sun-blackened, quarrelsome, he wondered sometimes whose children they were, Esau's, who was after all, the eldest?

Rachel was all he wanted, his seed through her thighs, instead he had been pushed forward in a goatskin by his mother, had to play the goat with Leah, Bilhah, Zilpah.

He was muttering after he threw them out, his sons, when they came with their next complaint, Joseph's dream.

"His dream!" Jacob shouted, starting up from the half sleep in which he listened, dozing, "His dream? Where are your dreams? You got none. You got brains like bulls, a thick bleeding piece of meat between your eyes; Reuben, Simon, Judah, Issachar, you ever have a dream in your life? That's my fault? Did I fuck a cow? Are these my kids? God, tell me, are these bastards mine?"

81

Bad words. It wasn't my father's fault his life was dreamless. It didn't mean his nose wasn't long, sensitive. He came home and sulked. All he ever wanted was a good word from his father. Didn't he spoil Er and me and the little one, Shelah? He threw the cushions right and left, crying, pulling at his black beard. "Fuck his cows," he screamed. "I'm through. Let him limp out of that tent and take care of things. I'm through with this shit. Hand up a kine's ass every day. Sheep piss in my hair. Enough. Let him run this show. Am I slave labor?"

A joke. Jacob was right.

My uncles, father, had no imagination. They staged a one-day walkout, then got sick with worry, somebody might be out there slipping a few sheep away on the sly, at night they heard a lion roaring at the herd's edge, wolves, cursing their husbandry, they shuffled out fast the next day to make sure Jacob's stock was safe, well-watered, moving in accustomed rounds, place to place.

I stood there at the door of mist. The damp sweat of the vision in the hollows of my cheek, under my lip.

Three

And Onan knew that the seed would not be his: and it came to pass, when he went in unto his brother's wife, that he spilled it on the ground, lest he should give seed to his brother. And the thing he did was evil in the sight of the Lord.

Genesis 38: 9-10

Rabbi Tanhuma said in the name of Rabbi Eleazar: In the hour when God created the first Adam, He created him as a golem and he was stretched out from one end of the world to the other . . .

Genesis Rabbah

Man, as he was before his fall, is conceived as a cosmic being which contains the whole world in itself and whose station is superior even to that of Metatron, the first of the angels. Adam Ha-Rishon, the Adam of the Bible corresponds on the anthropological plane to Adam Kadmon, the ontological primary man . . . . *Since Adam was truly and not merely metaphorically all embracing, his fall was bound likewise to drag down and affect everything. The Universe falls, Adam falls* . . . .

. . . *the first being which emanated from the light was Adam Kadmon, the "primordial man." Adam Kadmon is nothing but a first configuration of the divine light* . . . . *He is therefore the first and highest form in which the divinity begins to manifest itself* . . . . *From his eyes, mouth, ears and nose, the lights* . . .*burst forth* . . . . *Since however, the divine scheme of things involved the creation of finite beings and forms each with its own allotted place in the ideal hierarchy, it was necessary that these isolated lights should be caught and preserved in special "bowls"* . . . .*What really brought about the fracture of the ves-*

*sels was the necessity of cleansing the
elements . . . to give a real existence
and separate identity to the power of
evil.*

Jewish Mysticism
Gershom Scholem

Red, the dust of all that desert there, congealed into an
Adam, red man rising shaky out of the water and clay, his
thing, the women giggling as they spoke, big enough to cram
between the moon and sun, force the universe apart, cheeks
glowing over the cooking coals, rubbing, huddling into the
fire, flame in their mouths, "*Bubbameisers*," my grandmother cried, splashing a pot of water on them.

Still they whispered, stories Rachel had taught them,
nibbling the golden nose of her father's idol, picking its
nostril, even Leah laughed as the first man grew beyond the
furthest point of light, beyond the black night, shrank back
to this world, curling his smoking feet in oceans, seas,
mountains ribbing his back, even peaks pebbles in his
buttocks.

I sighed, limp, dying, breaking up into a thousand grains,
the impulse dead in me.

My stroll over, an empty universe, rock, clay, water; the
far off explosions of fire, lakes of gas I put my foot in,
feeling the heat and cold of vapor, veins of strange substance
and the crashing of spheres but none which I could not
overleap, make myself larger; or striding through the coverlet
of stars, mixing my fingers in the tangled clot of chaos,
howling at the edge, and stepping off only into deeper
emptiness.

85

I die now on this world where I first rose and took shape, dwindling smaller than the smallest star, no bigger than a moon, my red clay glutting a few valleys and hill sides. I lost it, whatever I imagined would be found in that first giddy swelling. Absorbing iron, gold, silver into the strata of my ribs, the hammer beating my temples, the chisel's final kiss at my lips, the slow turning into flesh, all these at the command of the beam which shone out through my eyes, touching all objects with sight. Was I not grand, the red man, striding over the sea of spheres, stepping from one to another rock in the streams of time, that cycle of decay I set going like a dial maker, spinning the flaming balls, pinching elements together, straining and mixing, a baby at play?

Delighting in all things, discovering the principle of each, the novelty of combinations, the shifting logic of possibility as each grew smaller and larger under my eyes, a vast box of toys, until I touched myself.

How could I see time created through my fingers and not wonder if the principle lay dormant even in the clay hulk I sat and pondered in?

Yes, then, frantically I began the search, thrusting my stone fingers into the mud vessels of my stomach, probing the large empty spaces of my skull, delving in the light chamber among the crevices for an answer. Learning their patterns, resealing the tiny rooms until poking my thumb there I could make my ankles twitch. A trick.

No answer there. Nor in the pumps and stoppers of the flesh I tore out of my chest and scrutinized, holding the wind within me as I figured out its works.

I scattered fingers, kneecaps, eardrums, nail bed, pulling the tiniest assemblies apart. How could it be helped, I came

86

at last to that appendage: loose and useless it seemed between my legs.

Already it had poisoned me, a spore in my bowels when I began to grasp my wrist, neck, heart. I held up but a shapeless sack of flesh or perhaps there was nothing there and I molded it out of a flap of skin, wanting something else, there at the crux of the body, upper and lower, a hole, another mouth, or the first mouth; or a tool to thrust into a mouth, darkness I imagined to drive myself forward.

It stiffened. How long I sat there, bored, wasting in the fever of tedium that had come upon me I can not tell, but now as it pressed, dazed, maddened, thinking the strain sickly sweet, was the touch of someone out of the emptiness; I embraced my own body, sun, moon, stars, bursting as the light broke, streaming out.

Crashing back upon the earth.

I know I am not alone. It is beyond me now to stop or put it back again, a husk. Clay was my constituent. It was a gift, the light. I break up into stones of iron, brass, a flood of sand out of my side and only this slow trickle of glass still molten from the sparks that flee outward illuminates, allows me a last few seconds. Time. I can measure it now for myself, how we decay. We—where is that other presence which broods above me? Delight I called you and seeing, stretching across the spaces did I not feel you animate my nature? Now leaving me, the seat of cold seeps out upon my ossified extremities.

Trapped in time and dying. I have memories now to torment me, of what was, will be, but make no sense of it. Separation. That's what you feel, Onan, lying here, the heartbeat under the red clay. Like me, your hand touched a fearful breach. Beware of yourself. Seek others. The presence was with me, trembling and penetrating the wet mud, shaping me to its pleasure and I bore it off mantled in joy to the furthest boundary I could imagine. A thousand shapes I was and were with me. I sought what you have, door, gate for those worlds that I had known were there and now, the shadow thickening in my skull, I saw . . . .

I was too weak to hold the light inside and enter time. Hollow I was and made of dust.

Put your fingers in me, Onan, feel the grains between your forefinger and thumb. Time is what you stroke, my body in it. Dreams will not carry you out of the weft. Desire is what you want. Better to crawl like Reuben into his father's bed. Hunger for what you can touch.

Better blood than seed on your hands—better to cut the throat and taste life bubbling in than know the sad separations of dream and its dross.

Onan, gather me, gather me up, restore the sparks that cling even to these shards, red, crumbling under your belly. Feel me. Your grandfather caught an angel in his sleep and wrested light away.

"No," I cried. "No, Golem." I wept, feeling the breast sway under my feet, the huge shape of the world molded into man, turning, buckling below me. "I can not hold the light I have. Look I am almost empty."

"Lie down with me then," the Golem whispered. "I will make love to you."

Four

*And Dinah, the daughter of Leah,
whom she had borne unto Jacob, went
out to see the daughters of the land.
And Shechem, the son of Hamor the
Hivite, the prince of the land, saw her
and humbled her. And his soul did
cleave unto Dinah, the daughter of
Jacob, and he loved the damsel, and
spoke comfortingly unto the damsel.
And Shechem spoke unto his father,
Hamor, saying: "Get me this damsel to
wife." Now Jacob heard that he had de-
filed Dinah, his daughter; and his sons
were with his cattle in the field: and
Jacob held his peace until they came.
And Hamor, the father of Shechem,
went out unto Jacob to speak with him.
And the sons of Jacob came in from the*

*field when they heard it; and they were
very wroth, because he had wrought a
vile deed in Israel in lying with Jacob's
daughter, which thing ought not to be
done.*

Genesis 34: 1-7

The sun withdrew from the night, blushed through the pale sky. Streaks of it awoke me where I lay embracing the red clay of the hill, my head nuzzled in a sand pit. Strapping my sandals on, drawing my white cloak about me, I stole back to my tent, tiptoeing, afraid I would meet those early risers, my strict, cruel uncles, Simeon and Levi.

My grandmother had kept her mouth shut about those sheets. She knew what was going on in my tent now. Impossible to keep her out of your business, she bustled everywhere, shaking her finger. Still she kept those two hypocrites off my back, self-appointed warders of the camp. Jacob couldn't stand them. He barred them from his tent. They skulked, furious, self-righteous, frightened, quarrelsome, haggling with everyone, in love with their sister.

No secret to anyone but them. That made them angrier, the teasing of their younger brothers, the smirks of the women, their father refusing to look at them, Leah's scorn. Look what we did! they shouted, happy as kids the day they came in with a cartload of bodies, the heads hacked off. We wiped them out! Dinah was weeping on the seat between them. The whole town. We leveled it. Whoo hah! Look at this, Simeon howled, hacking at the midsection of one of the torsos. Ain't it ugly? He threw a bleeding meat into the road where we were all gathering. They were sore. Heee Heeee. They were walking around like cripples when we got them.

90

Shechem's Dinah stood up screaming. Her husband's blood ran down her face from the black coil of her hair. Simeon and Levi grinned stupidly blinking in the early morning sun. Dinah was half naked, ripped out of Shechem's bed, his throat cut in a flurry of bed clothes, her brothers staring with greed at the sight of her as their knives plunged and fountains of crimson spouted at arm's length, jerking to and fro.

"Dad," they cried. "Dad. Look. Come out and look." Eyeballs glazed and fixed past the wailing women to the tent where the servants were waking him. Another wagon had come up with their servants driving it, furniture, crockery. Behind it we could see the dust rising in a column as the burning town's sheep and cattle were driven toward the camp.

"Dad! Dad!" they shouted.

Reuben, Judah, Dan, Asher ... tumbled out, half asleep, squinting at the golden vessels on the cart, the hammered-out obscenities of Shechem's household, gods squirming into each other's orifices, laughing, the blood of their masters dripping over their cheeks, bellies, upsprung cocks, over-spread thighs, jutting kneecaps. Reuben touched the gilded toe of one, extended out to him, and the clever assemblage of Shechem began to move, the gold idols crawling over one another, tongue to anus, elbow out of vagina, foot to ear, in and out upside down head to tail, the tiny men, women, bulls and monsters copulated as the whole pile came slowly crashing off the cart, almost upsetting it.

"Dad! Dad!"

The women had hustled Dinah into her father's tent. Jacob was up. You could see the stirring in the tent folds. We waited. All you could hear was a buzz from the interior and ominous sounds above as shadows swooped lower and lower over Simeon and Levi.

"Dad!" they called, their voices strained. "Dad!"

The crowd shuffled in the dust. Reuben left them first. Eying the flock sailing over them, he backed off from the rubble of idols around his feet, stepping over dented statuary, his sandals slapping in the silence, he disappeared under the flap. Asher shrank off next. My father then and Dan, Issacher, Zebulon . . . leaving them by themselves sitting on the cart seat. Leah appeared at the door of Jacob's goatskin house to shoo us in, away, not even shaking her finger at the two sons who stood helplessly holding the reins deserted by the servants too, alone with their booty—arms beating as they tried to drive off the glittering black wings that wheeled about their wagons, soaring and streaking, gobbets of flesh torn away, excrement dropping over the wagons, Simeon, Levi, white filth boiling and popping in the broiling sun as the vultures came down for the feast and in the stillness of Jacob's tent all of us kneeling, his lips moving in prayer, we listened to their screams.

Then we fled. He pulled up the tent stakes, combed through our grandmothers' luggage, throwing out the idols, pictures, statuettes, charms, amulets, all the souvenirs they had hauled off from Laban, buried them. We yanked down tents, strapped poles to our camels, drove in sheep, cattle, horses, and, loading up supplies, moved out.

Simeon, Levi hung on our rear. They had followed everybody into the river, washing themselves, changed their clothes, mumbled along in the prayers, and now, afraid to talk, afraid the old man might beat them off, they followed when Jacob saddled up. "Beth El!" he whooped. "Beth El!" the silver streaming out of his caftan as he galloped suddenly to the head of the caravan out of our old encampment. On all sides we heard the drums and horns of the Canaanites and

Perrizites, the cousins of Shechem, which burned behind us, mournful and menacing, spreading the news of the massacre. We marched with spears at the ready, servants armed to the teeth, braced for the hosts of Shechem's sister towns to fall upon us as the stink we had caused spread through the land. Jacob rode ahead of us all, his sons afraid to come near him, unarmed, white robes alight in the sun, hooves striking sparks on the stony trail, charging up the valley into a strange stillness which muffled the beat of our steps, jingling of the harness, creaking of the yoke and oxen as we rushed after him, not a sound from the whole train strung out over half a mile but his whoop goading his horse, "Beth El! Beth El!"

*   *   *

So we reached the oak of weeping. Deborah, Rebecca's nurse, died and we buried her under it. The old lady was ancient. She dated from Abraham and Sarah. A Methuselah. Laban's daughters were sick about it. Leah sulked around and Rachel who was pregnant cried day and night. Jacob insisted everyone call him Israel. Simeon and Levi, seeing no one was after us, insufferable again, shuffling about, boasting that the land was scared stiff, but staying out of their father's way who was setting up pillars, proclaiming new rules, a new life, bustling about like a patriarch. Bethel! The end of it was Rachel had an awful time in labor and, giving birth to Benjamin, died.

We had ridden between two files up the valley, Perizzites, Girgashites, Jebusites, Canaanites, Hivites, a bronze forest with iron leaves, the whole of it frozen in salt, the wind whipping their faces, shattered capitals, insignia eroding, they marched backward before Jacob stabbing themselves, overturning chariots, mangling their ranks: awoke bloody and dazed in their city squares regarding their wounds with amazement, sinking back to houses and beds in nightmare.

So it was over. Something. It had changed. Israel collapsed, stuck to his tent. His sons took over. Leah turned old overnight. Reuben crept into Bilhah's tent. Jacob said nothing. Simeon and Levi crept about the outskirts, ordering everyone, obnoxious, their older brother too guilty to assert himself and lay down the law.

I crouched behind a bush, slipping from its shadows as I saw their backs recede, the drab black sackcloth flapping, two ungainly earthfast birds circling the camp, their talons dragging in the dust, kicking the gravel, disappearing among the donkeys hobbled on the western edge. I jumped back into the circumference of the dogs, too familiar a scent to be barked at, and hurried toward my bed.

All the camp asleep, I wheeled at my door to see if I was unobserved and met it, burning, hot and pink, its damp touch making me shrink. All was seen, known. I knew, sudden, why they buried the old witch and prophetess under the weeping oak. Jacob changed his name, forgot his tricks, remained alone abjuring wives. And I had inherited a secret.

Reuben, Issachar, my father Judah, Dan, Zebulun, Asher, Gad, Naphtali, Benjamin, Joseph, even Simeon and Levi, would go one way, I another. Like Dinah hugging a memory between her sticky hams. "He humbled her," the brothers shouted. The women shook heads, afraid to show smiles; Shechem, his handsome snub-nosed face, blonde locks, touching their elbows as they bent at the common well, offering to draw the bucket up, bearing it, walking them home along a side path where they stop to rest, a soft spot in the gravel, sand, brushing away nettles and pebbles as he jokes and whispers, reaching out to draw back the shawl from their cheek, seeing the breast dug peeping from the blouse, swelling as he draws closer and his hand is dropping to their knee caressing it, reaching under the folds, tickling as if in play, as only half jumping away they entangle, seeing through this toss, unbuckled, the strange hooded snake slithering in his silken pants, whimpering, "Oh Shechem, no . . . oh . . . oh . . . no . . . no . . .", their sweat, burning, pink, the ancient sun explodes in them.

And lifting the tent flap, observing the crumpled bed-clothes in the corner, smelling the musty rankness of the goat's hair in which I would huddle sleeping away the black boiling heat of the day, hearing her heavy snoring—on hands and knees making my way to the blankets at the opposite end to curl, I . . . I felt the sun forcing its way down through the folds, oh . . . Shechem . . . no . . . no . . . ."

I smiled too.

Five

Fifteen cubits upward did the waters prevail; and the mountains were covered. And all flesh perished that moved upon the earth, both fowl, and cattle, and beast, and every swarming thing that swarmeth upon the earth, and every man, all in whose nostrils was the breath of the spirit of life, whatsoever was in the dry land, died. And He blotted out every living substance which was upon the face of the ground, both man, and cattle, and creeping thing, and fowl of the heaven: and they were blotted out from the earth; and Noah only was left, and they that were with him in the ark.

Genesis 7: 20-23

. . . after the primordial light was withdrawn there was created a "membrane for the marrow," a k'lifah, and this k'lifah expanded and produced another. As soon as this second one came forth she went up and down till she reached the "little faces." She desired to cleave to them and to be shaped as one of them, and was loth to depart from them. But the Holy One, blessed be He, removed her from them and made her go below. When He created Adam and gave him a partner, as soon as she saw Eve clinging to his side and was reminded by his form of the supernal beauty she flew up from thence and tried as before to attach herself to the "little faces." The supernal guardians of the gates, however, did not permit her. The Holy One, blessed be He, chid her and cast her into the depths of the sea where she abode until the time that Adam and his wife sinned. Then the Holy One, blessed be He, brought her out from the depth of the sea and gave her power over all those children, the "little faces" of the sons of men, who are liable to punishment for the sins of their fathers. She then wandered up and down the world. She approached the gates of the terrestrial paradise, where she saw the Cherubim, the guardians of the gates of Paradise, and sat down near the flashing sword, to which she was akin in origin. When she saw the flashing sword revolving,

she fled and wandered around the world and, finding children liable to punishment, she maltreated and killed them. All this is on account of the action of the moon in diminishing her (original) light. When Cain was born this k'lifah tried for a time without success to attach herself to him, but at length she had intercourse with him and bore spirits and demons. Adam for a hundred and thirty years had intercourse with female spirits until Naamah was born. She by her beauty led astray the "sons of God," Uzza and Azael, and she bore them children and so from her went forth evil spirits and demons into the world. She wanders about at night time, vexing the sons of men and causing them to defile themselves.

. . . Said R. Simeon, "Alas for the blindness of the sons of men, all unaware as they are how full the earth is of strange and invisible beings and hidden dangers, which could they but see, they would marvel how they themselves can exist on the earth."

The Zohar: Genesis

It was the waters that overwhelmed them. All the fountains of the great deep broken open, the windows of the Heavens rattled with the blast of rain. Upper world and lower world which they had put themselves between with spells, curses, anagrams, rushed together, a clap, a mighty wave, blotted all.

It was the earth which was corrupt. Not just man, uplifted speck of clay, or his brothers, animals that ran four-footed, or birds that flew above him, even clusters of insects that swarmed, or finally seed sprouting in humus, rot, up into the blighted barley and wheat, but corruption had seeped into the very salt crystal, sand, splinter of rock so that the whole of it, curved and shuddering obscenely, stank in the eye.

So we can hardly imagine that generation. It started with Adam's disgust, Eve. After Abel's death he couldn't look at her. He had heard all this talk of sin, evil, crime but it meant nothing, too confusing, hard to grasp, he took a bite in a bad apple, wasn't even a taste to that fruit. They'd been punished. He was afraid. Something done that wasn't supposed to be, but too thin for him to smell, touch, taste.

Then the blood, losing—the word death the angel had uttered palpable. And he looked between Eve's legs where Abel and Cain had come from and it was ugly. He got down on his knees and sniffed it. The smell was awful, not as he had thought it before. He saw stretch marks on her tummy, her breasts drooped, that black bush where he thought sometimes he might slip back down into the garden, now stank of blood, sweat, piss, seemed like the gate to that place, death. And he was afraid. He stayed away from her. Slept by himself.

She came. Mist, fine air, perfume of clover blossom, iris, lily, split herself in two, a sister. They lay down beside him with gauzy limbs rubbed along his body, fluttering, drawing the sweetness out of her pistil, sucking until his temples hammered with joy and he swooned, "Enough! Enough!" at their ticklings leaving his body rosy, a host of tiny creatures like herself taking wing from each spore of the lump, seed, he threw up, progeny of Lillith, first wife of the first Adam, that clay man under them both, flying off to copulate like flies, seeking out not only Cain but bears, lions, calves, trees, flowers, even the cleft of the rock.

Cain! Cain! The cursed one, and the smell of murder, scorpions, toads, snakes, scurrying out of the way, turning on the sand as he hears the soft giggling call of girls behind him and sees them hanging back a few yards, suddenly bashful, trying to stuff breasts back in the thin stuff of their dresses, drawing the veil, mischievous, across faces.

His sister, a twin, among them and he feels the mark on his forehead fiery, the sweat of his brow scalding drop by drop as she too skips showing her long girlish legs, the length of them up to her waist as the desert wind whips their skirts lifting them . . . they dart about him, just out of touch. He cries, a bitter voice, is this his punishment, faint as the spike of hunger goes through him, comes out between his legs as he speaks her name, Naaah, Naaah, the seed in his hands only it is not his sister who is standing in front of him now, her blue eyes watching him steadily over the edge of the half veil which outlines the chisel of her nose and chin. The smell of flowers, soft yellow puffs, a carpet of them. He strikes at her but the fingers touch his just as he swings down and the cool stroke stops him, he can't help it as the hand reaches out, he does feel it and is dazzled, so icy, the seed pumps from him again and again as she strips off the bandages from her glowing olive face, the soft red berries of her lips helping him to find the apple breasts, pear buttocks, purple flesh of the dark plum its veined flesh between his teeth, he can not hold her, eat her, die within her enough. Her wrappings are off, throttled between her legs, squeezing, trying to possess the quick, laughing creature, he aches, Cain, he is sick, as the shape draws off him filled with his creation, his shining grandmother, first Eve, the *k'lifah.*

The sand is wet and scummy under his feet as he stands, shaky. His forehead is cold. He has lost something. Now he is alone and for the first time since his hands struck out at Abel, he shivers.

"Momma," he cries. "Momma."

*　　*　　*

Foliage took root under him, twisted out of the damp, seeping down into the dust. "Maaah! Maaah!" Green shoots of grass as broad as Cain's palm, trees towering over him so high he could not see the tops, the crash of their spores, fruit, nuts, like rocks. Orange, violet, massy blossoms sprang out of the moist turf, their stalks curling in grotesque loops, grapes as big as his head ripened on the vines that clung and wound about the swollen trunks crowding each other out of the vast forest. Sap, honey, the scent of fermenting liquor thick and sticky, gobs of it clinging to his hands, feet, hair.

"Cain, Cain," the cloying voice licking at him. She was descending. He tried to turn away from her but his eyes misted and again the snow of her flanks as she settled on him drove the rusting bolt up. He dissolved in her black coiling hair, tasting nothing, nothing.

Perfume, he reached out through the fog, tried to bite into her calf, knee, but eluding him, slippery, she lashed out drawing up what was left, specks of pleasure, playing with flaccid nipples, stroking his earlobes, licking the trickle of clear fluid from his organ's tip. And he shuddered, shook, the whole of him vibrating like a stick, brittle, thinking he was going to crack in two, snap, as she came down again upon him, her fingers in the gut of his bowels, twanging their

101

strings as he was forced to squeeze the very last film of his dreams from the glands into her bowl, gripped not in an embrace of sweetness now but in dry rush of heat, cracking his lips and tongue as she seared—turning him round and round, whirling him over her flames, singeing his hairs—searching the final drop.

Stopped, dry as ash, he was still now like a cinder, clear except for the wet burning dream that clutched him, lying by his side. "Go! Go!" he begged.

He heard her laugh.

"Go! Go!"

It hurt as she drew off him, the pain not in his flesh but in the clarity of light, sharpening the edges of rushes, splintering rocks, razoring the minute details in the nubble of the moss which sprang up when he rose on his elbow, hoping as his eyes cleared—the flood ebbed away, streams of it into the spongy earth—that all was shrunk like himself to smallness again.

He started forward, yet in his nose, throat, eyelids, bone marrow he is being tugged again, away, away from the earth, he fights, shaking his head, trying to knock himself against the air awake for it is changing, the sand between his thumbs, dreams are coloring the substance between his fingers, everything is losing its presence, hardness, he can not grip it any more. He does not know now if he is asleep. He opens his eyes.

He is where his fingers told him he was when he lost his hold.

In sand.

There is nothing but sand. It is hot yet as he sifts it through his fingers there is that sick feeling that it is not real.

The edge of the sand is gone though his fingers and toes are blistered with its heat.

He stands up, blinking.

The sun is shattering panes of silver below him. He puts his hand out so that the brilliance of reflection there shall not wash out his sight. A fire too bright to observe, the sparks blue and green fly off the edges of it. He hears the scream. Then in his ears becomes aware of a high, hardly audible music, singing, that makes his nostril and forehead ache and looking for an instant over the edge of his little finger catches sight of the silhouette of a wing, a shadow like a sheet of mica, glistering with the body of the sun and then the low undulating throb that drums in the sands coming up through ankle and femur like a heartbeat making the hillside tremble.

The scream again. He knows that voice. Shading his eyes, he tries to peer into the silver furnace. The sheets of mica flicker, ten, twelve, twenty, he can not count. The outline of a body.

"Uuuu . . ." she is crying out. Her voice brittle, strung so taut her chords must break if she goes up another note, vibrating with awful pleasure. "Uuuuuzz . . . uuuuzzz. . . uzza!" It stops, the human voice, but the singing goes on.

His eyes sting. Through a crack in his fingers he can see shadows, a snaking line in the cauldron of liquid light. It flows together, parts, breaking off in two, three.

"Aaaaa . . . aaaaa . . ." It starts again, her hysterical moans. "Azzzzz . . . ."

It is her. He squeezes his thumbs into his sockets against the pain of the reflection. Yet her body is only a moon to their corruscation, throwing off the beams, and he has seen it for a second clearly, a black glowing coal, the full tense

103

breasts and buttocks, the young firm flesh he has lusted for now poisoned with holiness.

She can not hold their seed. It overflows her tiny slit, runs down her thighs, a spreading puddle under her, fills the hollow of the valley, a lake of glittering mercury, floats them up as they circle her swimming in their own silver sperm.

The light is dimming now. Their wings drag, dampened in the shining sea of angelic scum. Still he must squint at them through the latticework of his fingers, the two cherubim frolicking round, diving, leaping up, carrying her aloft a few feet, dipping her down into the molten sweetness that their delicate members had bubbled like uprushing springs into her narrow trough, and in their center spinning, a slow wobbling top, her legs outspread, crying for more, "Uzzzaa . . . Azzzaellll . . ." his sister, child, Naamah.

The sea of perfumed silver shimmers in rainbows, touches his foot and giddy, he falls backward, shielding his eyes, fainting, his mouth open.

*   *   *

It is not what you can touch, he thinks as his head clears. The light is burning down on him, his head. There is nothing in his throat but thirst. His lips are black. Water. I want water. There is no woman, angels, in the valley, only a few lumps of pitch. The ground is hot. He finds a shriveled snakeskin, scabs. Water! Water! He runs up the side of the hill and sees the same sandy depression in front of it. Water . . . . He runs down again and up. Water. He can almost taste it in the dried cracks of his lips. Water . . . to stop the sand that is blotting him against the sun. Sand stinging, choking, clotting him. Sand into which he is sinking like a plummet. Dragging himself up from its waves for one last leap, and again, and again. And he sees it, over the rim of the next ridge, and the next ridge. Water. He runs down, up, down, up, toward . . . so blue. Like some well of the sky itself. The blue robe of the power. And he falls to kiss the hem, to clutch the fringe threads. I kiss you. I adore you. I taste you. Taste you. The blue water comes trickling into his mouth. And with horror he realizes it is real. Through the salt he tastes, water, water.

Later they find him at the edge of the lake, his great great great grandson's daughter's children, nephews. He recognizes the family features, long hooked nose, small ears, blunt teeth, the upright walk. No, they are not beasts although the huge arm, the hand as big as his whole body, frightens him. They move with large, unwieldy steps. He is afraid they will kill him but careful of his smallness, slowly, cautiously, they lift him up under their nose, pass him round.

They boomed at him. Fingers in his ears, he heard them speaking of his sister or great great great great granddaughter, the tiny mother from whose legs they crawled one after another buckling her body in maddening cramps so that she cursed her huge issue, hulking, pushing them away from her tits where they hung like a litter of dogs. Other brothers and sisters they had too, they told him, their soft thunderous voices filled with wonder, massive children, winged things of gauze that fled into the sky, red crawling shapes, two-headed, five-legged spawn glimmering with golden scales, fish tails that crept off to the water, copper creatures who buzzed like flies, tiny men with the ears of bats.

And they spoke of their uncles, the hairless men of Adam's seed who came to fornicate and feast among their sisters, oily bodies so white and slippery they wriggled on each other's private parts, giggling, trying to eat each other's flesh.

105

And there was a snake bigger than anything they had ever seen, and they had never seen it all, that came up, rearing snout and forked tongue, breathing brimstone, from the ocean depths. Stranger beings, all fire and color who dropped down from the skies. And the skies opened and closed with rumblings. Streams burst from the earth and mounted up high to disappear.

"And," he cried out, shouting, a strangling in his throat, "are there ones like me?"

"Oh yes, a few, Seth's brood."

"And your mother?"

Maaaah, Maaaah, Maaaah . . ." They set up a wailing that almost cracked his head in two. She would not talk to them.

"Naamah . . . Naamah . . ." Whispering the name Cain found himself on fire. He wanted her. Mounting the shoulders of her oaf sons, he called for them to take him to her camp. They trundled off.

Holes in the ground, deep caverns underneath the earth they had dug, burrowing like moles in long culverts. At the bottom with a stick, they poked a further passage for their mother's chamber, deeper than their eyes could see, lit first by her glowing body but now dark. He took a bit of coal from their cooking fire, an ash. "Naamah? Naamah?" he called, picking his way down the tunnel over the rocks.

He touched a carpet of silken yarn. He floated forward. And there at the back of the chamber he saw the three, a spider's nest between the socket of her thighs, the angels' skins, hers, hanging in shreds of leather to whitening bones, three souls fluttering helplessly under fleecy dripping wool, the opulent strings of cobweb.

The mark burned on his forehead and he wept. He foresaw his own death, the arrow of her father Lamech, his

106

descendant, in his throat, the blood spilling out, at last the long journey over or begun. The sweet rot of red filled up his mouth as he dreamt of seeing Abel again. Seven hundred years was too long to live.

*   *   *

Was it Enoch who caused it? Enoch who seeking Cain sought to understand the invisible as well as the visible world, collecting the secrets of generation, calling upon his ancestor, the ancient Adam, six hundred and fifty years old, to speak of the mysteries in the Garden, taking down the words of Uzza and Azael as they shriveled into dust, learning the secret names of the presences, tapping the streams of light that bubbled in the earth, setting down the language of the leaves, birds, summoning the demons to his aid, befriending the angels.

While his nephews, nieces, cousins, children, children's children, all but one of the issue of his loins were swarmed in murder, adultery, sodomy, bestiality. Leaning over his shoulder, reading the leaves, they became skilled in the divination of the spirits. Some lay with cattle in the field, garlanding the bull's horns, perfuming the cow's hind-quarters. Others fell in love with trees, entreating sap from the oak, maple, cherry; grafting their human flesh into the branches. Others shaped partners from the earth itself, molding the clay into breasts, mouth, arms, manipulating the likeness of their sleeping fantasies, breathing quickness into the limbs. Aye, the earth itself—corrupt. Fetid with human blood, see, it steamed of heat, and man lay down upon his ancient mother and made love to her. Death: when Enoch's fingers fell from the pages of the book, Methuselah turned them, seeking within the leaves that Adam brought out of the Garden, the pathway to his father and his father's father. And after him, Lamech, and Noah after him, the bright essences who danced about his chair and brought him stories of the upper, lower world could not enlighten man on that: one terrible key that had been turned to lock him out.

They raged, at last, the generation of the Flood. Stamped their feet upon the earth, abusing it, defiling it, deliberately, hoping the upper world would take notice. Cut their bodies, crippled themselves, refused to spawn with humankind, ate their babies. Stopped up fountains of goodness, mercy, drove off the angel that came down to plead with them. Death! Death! They were sick of it. They would pervert the whole world, upper, lower, real and dreamed, until they were set free. Noah! Free! Free!

What good was this turning of pages? Adam had died. Cain had died. Enosh was dead. Kenan, Mahalalel, Lamech, Mehuhael, Irad, Adah, Seth. And a whole numberless host.

What was the sin of the generation of the Flood?

They corrupted the earth.

Man sinned, why call the earth corrupt?

Man is the "essence of the earth", he can infect the earth with his own corruption.

Why were the animals extinguished too?

He had perverted them, even to the birds of the air, even the insects are of his foulness.

How?

He did not allow the upper and lower waters to "meet in conjunction", he intervened in all natural process, prevented its intercourse, his violence, abstract, overreaching, was impossible. The measure of sin was not filled up, however, until he destroyed his own seed.

108

If men, even their children, were skilled in magic and divination, how is it they had no foreknowledge of the Flood?

They did, but they thought they could avert the catastrophe as they were on good terms with the angel in charge of fire, and the angel in charge of water.

How did the Flood come about?

"Measure for Measure." Man had wasted his "warm fluid" upon the ground. So, bubbling up from below, "all the fountains of the Great Deep were broken open," hot, burning waters scalded him. From above, "and the windows of Heaven were opened," it fell in cold sheets. The giants stood upon the springs.

The manner of their death was as follows: scalding water spurted up from the abyss, and as it reached them it first burnt the skin from the flesh, and then the flesh from the bones, the bones then came asunder, no two remaining together, and thus they were completely blotted out.

Said God to them: "You wish to undo the work of my hands; your wish shall be fully granted, for every living thing that I have made will I blot out from the face of the earth. I will reduce the world to water, to its primitive state, and then I will form other creatures more worthy to endure."

109

Woe to those sinners, since they will not rise from the dead on the day of the last judgement . . . they were blotted out.

The Zohar

Six

What was Er's sin?

He had not crept like his uncle into a father's bed, tickling a giggling middle-aged handmaiden who turned and twisted, teaching him tricks while the other wives sulked against their pillows, hearing the gasps and shrieks. Jacob snored lost in thoughts of departed Rachel. There was no brother-in-law's blood bright on Er's fingertips as he tore at the roasted kid's meat, those crimson hands of Simeon and Levi. My careless older brother, too willing to fall in with his father's choice and marry. Who suspected—least of all that innocent, Judah, always the compromiser, the peacemaker, the arranger, hustling around the camp to make everyone happy, keep peace, not too pious but . . . Leah's favorite, Jacob's puppy, wagging his tail like a dog when his father threw him a word—the appetite of Er.

It was the old blood, Nimrod's running in us. Er had Esau's hairy arms, the hunter's that delighted in a thrust into the lion's bowels, scrapping of jackal jaws, the crazy red rush of the wild boar, yelling and hee-hawing as the arrow string snapped and the shaft sang and slammed its wooden note into fountains of the flesh. And Lot's eyes, shifting yellow pupils that looked on sin, drinking the city's foulness like tonic, glinting at the neighbor's stories of the latest unnatural act, just down the block, leaving off only at the final possible moment, his partner unable to resist, angels dragging them off by the elbow, a last hungry look at the sight of so many good nightmares and himself but half asleep, wine bubbling on his lips, salt of the night vision, as his daughters undid his bed clothes and licked his sex awake, impaling themselves on father. Father! Father! "And he knew not when they lay down and when they rose up."

There was no need to look to my mother's pedigree for explanations of those three mutilated ewes, their white wool spotted with the drippings of their arteries, feet hobbled, private parts enlarged. The herdsmen pointed to them laughing. "A buggerer! Someone in the camp was sick. Ha!" Jacob's sons looked at each other. It must have been one of the servants. Keep an eye out, they instructed. Those cut throats bothered them more.

An old puzzle, squawkless round the tent door had come headless chickens, three-legged dogs, one-legged pigeons, a fox stumbling in with its eyes pecked out, the mule whose tongue was cut off, the cat tied down and starved, a dish of sour milk just out of reach, its skeleton poking through a mangy coat, little spots of fur burned away.

After the ewes, Leah meddled. She knew our steps out of the cradle, her eyes on the infant who toddled back under the covers and the baby who crawled into the corner where he had been warned away, hoping to see the mouse, snake, spider, they threatened; witnessed the first pulling off of long legs, insect wings, muffled chuckling: stuck her big face in the excited, ruby cheeks, "Grandma?" and slapped them hard.

Her cure, responsibility, a partner, kids, the regular schedule, everything would straighten out. Look at Reuben,

Simeon, Levi, all that trouble, restlessness, best to nip it in the bud.

So my father went looking for a girl. His kind of girl, among his pals, Adullamites. Er was excited. He knew my father's taste, big tits, good ankles, a large ass but firm. Judah's eyes wandering around the camp, always alighted on the best of flesh. He couldn't help, laughed about it, even slapped his Ma's behind, playful, a horse and camel breeder, proud of his nose for animals, wasn't Jacob blessed with it, all those speckled lambs, breeding like crazy, streaked and grizzled under Laban's distraught gaze. Israel's fecund streak itched in Judah's fingers.

He was laughing when he brought her home. Right away they hit it off, the trick dancing under her lashes, teasing each other, wait till you see my son, he's what I used to be, ha, ha. She drew the veil across her face to hide her smile, embarrassed.

"Ain't she sweet! Ain't she *sweeet!*" Judah roared as they pulled into camp, Tamar hiding like a daughter under his arm. "Come on, honey. Come on, show your new momma your face. Come on," he said, lifting her up out of the cart, "Let everyone see that face."

She made sounds like a kitten but finally, everybody staring at her, she let the silk drop from her nose and lips.

"Wheeee . . ." Judah whistled. "Was I kidding? You ever see a bird so pretty?"

We all shifted about.

"Er??? Er???" Judah shouted.

"Take her inside," Leah called. "Don't keep her standing here like a camel."

We all laughed. Tamar too.

113

"Er, where's Er?"

Er slipped out of the crowd around the tent door.

And Er laughed too, slowly, his black eyes dimming, that low chuckle, throaty "heh, heh."

"You know what to do?"

The ground shook with merriment, whooping, haw-hawing, "Judah!" Grandmother was shouting over the din. "Judah! Get her inside."

The drums began, the goatskins, beating, beating, for the marriage. I was queasy in the stomach. The way she had looked around as she started to go inside the tent, staring at my father, me too, straight in the face, those frank eyes that would not stay still but danced, jumping from person to person, avoiding her bridegroom to be but smiling, half helpless, half knowing, until Leah whispering in her ear drew the veil across her face.

*   *   *

Drumming, drumming, under us, Er beside me shook. You could feel the heat coming off him, his nose red, as she drew back among the women, lifting her skirts above the rugs, showing her ankles. They were bringing the roasts, puddings, the sweet grease of lamb, crushed mint, pepper, saffron, poppy. The women opposite the men across the dishes. "Hey! Hey!" the herdsmen to the rear of the family exclaimed as the wineskins were passed out, squirting streams of the heavy sugar of fermented grape, exploding in their faces as they sucked, tore at their bread, sang out, "Hey! Hey!" The thrumming of the goatskins altered now from a quick erratic patter to the steady, hypnotic throb of the tent dance, the deep drums joining, the hides sucking in and out

114

and we heard the clink of the coins at their ankles and wrists, the head silver and the necklace, as they rose, the girls of the camp, across a table of steaming meats, bending low under the folds of the tent roof, swaying from side to side, their voices picking up the high keen of the flute and pipe, "aaaahh . . . aaaahh . . ." they called, letting their breasts slide to the music, "aaahh . . .", turning slowly so you saw the bounce of their nipples under the thin, holiday cloth and the profile of their erect tits, delicacy of their ankles, the roundness of their thighs; now they loose the locks of their hair, unbraid, and a flood of it black, brown, red, flowed loose under the goatskin awnings, waves of it whipping their faces as they turned, rolling with the drums now, the soprano stamping of their anklets teasing the bass-throated booming and the twist over and over of their backsides as they swayed, turning, turning, their buttocks writhing to the drummer's hands, round and round, hair flailing, skirts falling, rising, falling, "aaaahh . . . ." Now they shiver as they dance, quivering, revolve and goose bumps stand out upon their arms, lick the blood from their lips, a tremor as the drummers turn them slower and slower, dance in the shaking of legs, breasts, buttocks. And the sweat is breaking out on men's foreheads. My father motions Shelah, the youngest, to leave the tent, the wineskins forgotten, the meat cold. No one can stop the drummers now. We hear the voice of the goat in the hides, the crude call of the billy, its curling nose, the sneer of its lips, and the tremble of beard in the room. The men snort and paw the ground and the pipe whistles through their noses. "Aaaahh . . ." the shriek of the jackal and the calling of birds as the women face us, opening their half-closed eyes, looking as if woken from sleep or we, opening our eyes with them *in* sleep, look into their stare as the thump comes up in them, again and again; gathering it tight between their thighs, against their breasts, in the small of the back, armpits, hollow of the knee, neck, along their cheeks, nostrils, palms, fingertips, biting at it, "aaaahh . . . aaaahh . . . ." The drummers will not stop. They have to be dragged away from the skins, beaten awake. But it goes on, even after my father has stopped it, sent everyone home, it is still beating in me, the craziness long after the lights have been doused and the camp is in darkness and I understand Jacob's mistake now, the urgency with which Judah clutched my mother out of the row of married women, the hoarseness in my uncles' voices and I am afriad. Er, as he is led off to the tent to meet his wife, is crying. His face is white as the men push him, their faces black with blood, grunting.

The way they looked at us. It did not matter, Er, I, my father, legs buckling, almost touching the floor, open, open to that beat coming up into their bellies from the depth, a well, well, lashing with black hair and sticky sweetness round a hole. I would lose myself, forever. I heard the scream in the night. My brother refused to go.

*   *   *

Leah finally separated them. The girl was bleeding in the morning from the wrong place. Er was sick.

Too much wine, she told Judah. Though Er strutted around the camp in a few days and Tamar was covered with bite marks, the sickness clung to my brother. He could not eat yet his belly swelled. The knife was missing from his scabbard. Tamar smiled but said nothing, sticking close to Leah at the well. One day he did not come out of the tent and Leah brought her over to Jacob's quarters. "Until he gets well."

A month later Er was dead.

And the sickness was working in me. At the funeral, they were smiling, Judah, Leah, in my direction.

In that delirium, an odor trailing tendrils in the tent, not of leaf and flower, jasmine, lily, peppermint, but of an animal, the sour tickling perfume that bruised the eye and made one faint with its headiness, drawn up in the nostril until I can take the silver chink between my teeth and the locks of copper, crow hair are oily on my tongue.

The last shovelful drops on Er. My father takes my arm. "Onan . . ."

And my grandmother beaming at me, my stomach turns weak.

I do not hear them as they explain.

My father's hands red, calloused, not large but thick, inscribed with his labor, early rising to the herds, crouching in the pale gray before dawn over tiny fires, holding a steaming clay bowl, hot water for his empty stomach between those powerful fingers.

Sometimes as a child, four, five, I crawled out of the blankets stirred by the crackling of the wood chips in the flames, my heart beating fast, anxious that the giant, my father should be up before the day began, brooding over us.

I put my small palm next to his around the bowl as he bent it toward my mouth. But the water was flat, unsweetened, his taste for it a mystery like the size of his hand, thigh, something I could never encompass.

Even then I was stunted, not in size, rather the impulse roused me from the sheets then drew me back as if my father's world was something set apart. I had no knack with animals, the neighbor's tongue, Aramaean, Egyptian, lip of

Caanan were not fluent in my mouth, my hand as it grew remained delicate but not cunning beside his own.

Something in me did not grow to man. Of the ancient ones, they said they were hoary before they came to generation. Seth begat Enosh after one hundred and five years. Lamech lived one hundred eighty and seven years before he conceived Noah. And Noah waited five hundred before he gave his seed for Shem, Ham, and Japeth. Our thrice great grandfather Terah did not have children until he was seventy and my great great grandfather Abraham had to tarry until eighty-six for that wild ass Ishmael. Er was but a tender branch and I, a green sapling.

Jacob the breeder, his son Judah, quickening the rhythm of life in their tents, anxious for a multitude, a people, spreading out the tent cords.

He was still among his toys, Er, when they gave Tamar to him. She was a large new animal put under the covers, thing to play with, see if it was alive, when he put his knife out or the live coal.

To be touched, handled, made to crawl between her legs, turned away if he pressed too hard? Not Er, the hunter who crouched upon the lion's haunches, piercing its life with the bubbling spear.

My brother, older yet younger than me. Children were brought into Tamar's bed. My head full of fairy tales: at ninety, one hundred, gout in my legs, cataracts clouding my eye, I might have gripped a girl's flesh eagerly and renewed myself. Or if Tamar, like Sarah, had waited eighty years, a sister to me, for the miracle to dower her again with clear skin and a teen ager's lithe spring . . . I am still in fairy tales. This camp is ridden with them, a plague of wonders.

My father's hand upon my arm. I feel the strength still in

118

his fingers, holding me as he would a balky bullock or unbroken colt, running his left hand up and down my shoulder to quiet me, light, gentle, while his right hand holds me fast, "Your brother's name . . ."

He can't let go of that. Has his dreams too, solid ones, tribes like Jacob from his loins. Of all the old man's talk that makes sense best to him. A nation, the same luck with kids as sheep. Seed. It's only seed. Seed for your brother and the hand squeezed as if to pump my acquiescence.

Grandma is grinning on the other side. Forget the sheets is in her eyes. She's pinching me, her *boitchik*. Now is the time to wipe them clean, the family restored, a bit of slime, that's magic, eh, she winks. She knows what's in my head and don't I like Tamar, untouched it turns out, a virgin, she saw the looks between us in the tent, admit, admit?

No, No, I'm screaming with my mouth open but no sound comes out. I have to make a noise but they keep up on either side of me, quickening the step, brushing away the mourners come up to comfort us.

"A quiet ceremony, no noise, or . . . do you want, a big one?"—"Whatever makes him happy," the other voice chimes in.

"So," said Leah, good and loud, stopping us, thrusting her big body in our path, pulling my head down to her beaming face oozing joy, puffing out, breathing my air, suffocating, "It's straight."

She pulled at my cheek, wrestled me down between her sagging breasts, cradling me . . . yoy . . . yoy . . . hugging me breathless, weightless. Only it was an apple coming up in my throat, poisonous as I tried to bite through it to articulate, choking me in bile, no, no.

"Wonderful. Ha! Ha!" My father let go of my arm and

119

hobbled I went forward a few steps in Leah's grapple, tumbling over, down on the stony ground on top of my grandmother.

My father's laughter above me.

Seven

Isaac, his face pink, a child's threads of snow on his head, a drift of it burying his chin, breast, waist; blind he is held fast in the ice of one hundred and sixty years; the ancients, his two sons, over a hundred, approach his chair with awe.

He smiles as he hears the footsteps. His mouth puckers on a sweet. His cheeks are unwrinkled, gleaming. "Don't fool me," he calls out in his high, tremulous voice.

The two male children look at one another. "We're together," they rejoin. "It's both of us."

"No tricks?"

"No, Dad, no," they are giggling, shaking their heads of frost.

"You sure?" Isaac sucks the tip of his thumb. His face glows. He loves tricks. "Stay where you are," he commands, rubbing the thumb against his gums. "I want to guess."

The older clears his throat.

The younger blows his nose.

Isaac points to the right, "Jacob?"

The whole tent rocks with laughter. The pole behind Isaac's chair sways back. Esau puts out his hand to steady the cords above their heads.

"Again? I made a mistake?"

"It's me, pa!"

"Let me feel."

Esau gives his finger to his father, puts it against his cheek. Isaac sniffs. "Smells fishy."

The index and forefinger of his older son strokes his baby skin, the hairs of Esau thick as goat's, coarse, gray, curling, a thicket of them twisting around his knuckles, the calluses of his bow strings under the mat, blood of the hunt a brick red dye striping the silver.

"Jacob?"

"Pa, it's me."

"It's a goat."

"Pa, it's him," Jacob piped.

"Esau?"

"Yeah, Pa, it's me, Pa."

"How can I be sure?"

"It's *me*, Pa," Esau cried.

"Jacob?"

"Yeah, Pa."

"Let me feel."

Jacob puts his fingers to his father's other cheek, the slick hairless thumb and tapering digits, delicate as a girl's, double jointed, still alive with the suppleness of a wrestler, stroking the dimple by Isaac's lips.

"Oooh, it's smooth."

We are all leaning in, the tots, to listen, bouncing up and

122

down with glee because Isaac is only a blown up little boy, a white-haired comedian playing to the kiddies. The older children, Esau's, Jacob's issue, adolescents, are hanging back embarrassed by the games, forgetting days when they crawled over the old man's seat, searching for candy he secreted in folds of his coat. Our grandfathers visiting him separately to show off their broods, a swarm of tiny ones buzzing up and down on blind Isaac, a thick shrub of flowers, all perfume, swarming in his beard, pockets, under the hem of the robe, sniffing a sweet that drove one into fits, odor that clung to him, they say, after the sacrifice so that not even hairy Esau whose nose was in the blood of the field, urine of the hunting dogs, animal entrails, bowels of the stag, could tear himself long away from the aroma of his father, tickling the hairs above his angry red lips even as he scowled at his smooth brother, making him smile, silly as a baby suckling on his father's thumb.

"I am dying," Isaac said.

"No, Pappa."

"No, no," screamed Esau.

"Don't leave us, Pappa."

"I'm dying."

Esau was pulling at his father's fringes, tears bubbling up, entangling his fingers at the hem of the robe, clutching it, "Don't go. Don't go!"

"*Kindeh,* I've got to go."

Jacob was screaming now too. "No, no!"

"Shhhh . . . the kids are here. Get ready."

And now he took out his hands, those pink, chubby palms that Jacob and Esau dreaded and sought, from the folds of his robes he drew those arms that had not protested, raised themselves in horror to struggle when his father bound him

123

down on the crude altar stones, assembled slowly, the black boulders piled one on another as if Abraham were hauling the blocks of his own tomb, only half awake, hoping he had misheard, this spirit he had followed, hoping for justice, had commanded the blood sacrifice of Canaan from him, a first born son of Sarah, the same gift that the idols of the place demanded, images whose cousins he had smashed in Ur, the same sick jealousy he thought he had left on the other side of the river.

"Will you withold your only son from me?" That question had nagged him from the moment of birth, miracle, he had not dared to pray for, fruit out of her barren womb and now at least he had something of the faceless spirit which kept at him in his dreams and wanderings, something he could rest his eyes on and say, I *am* happy, not like Sarah's beauty which was always glimmering away, impossible to touch, taste, here a bit of a thing, an apple you could squeeze and tickle rosy any hour of the day and growing up the faces of Sarah and himself mingled, his seed, his soul, making light of death and the dark angel; the moment it came squalling out, thudded against his heart, the fear of the voice that spoke to him. "Will you give it over?" calling to him in the night vision he shook off as the dregs of wine. Will you? Will you? This bastard land, each tree and rock whispering in your ear. He had forbidden it in the camp, tilling of the earth with children's bodies, pounded into the compost; defied the little gods of the furrow whose mouths the locals claimed lusted after the bones and gristle of Canaan's infants before they shat out heavy ears of grain, the fat of wheat, pissed winepopping from the grapes, streams of honey in the rock: and now the voice, mocking, teasing, drew him on to give it everything, everything.

The odor of the spices made him faint, frankincense, myrrh, reeking, a jar must have broken or the flames were licking at the chips of resin. Had he gone through it then, the sun was smoking on his knife, Isaac lay still below him, was it over, God?

No, the boy's neck was whole, the heat was in his brain, he had gone through the moment and come back, now, now, or never and he swung to stab.

Hands! Hands! They filled the room, glowing, brilliant, caught the great gold fish of the sun and shone its scales as mirrors through the tent. Isaac was blessing them, his sons. The child who had been lifted up into Heaven by the angels burning, a savour under the nose of the Unknown while his shadow lay bound on the stones below (for I too require something of man, of that echo of myself in him, that will to do what he calls holiness, not his hysteria or his first fruits but the very bone of him so I may rib myself). So now not only the odor of the altar but the light of it burst around us in the tent as Isaac raised those palms, pink and fiery, to sanctify his seed.

Isaac! Isaac! The children, grandchildren, I among the babies, wept, hearing that he was going. We ran, the little ones to his skirts, trying to hold onto the cloth as if his soul were wind that we could pin down to the earth. He was smiling. "I'm here. I'm here," he whispered, patting our fingers, hands, pushing candies into our mouths. "Shhhhh . . . I'm still here."

Why did you arise from us, O Ancient? Sometimes I wake up in the morning and smell you in the covers, that sweetness and I shake the wrappings from the bed thinking that I will kiss each thing in the world for the first time through the dew. I feel the waterbeads trembling in my hair. I see you

125

smiling in the tent door. What is Jacob's magic, Joseph's rainbow to the clear blue happiness in your eyes? Isaac! Isaac!

When they carried his body to the cave where his father and mother lay, no one in the camp was bitter. His light shone even in Er's face and my uncles Simeon and Levi. Esau's people joined their hands to ours and sat in ashes and sackcloth not crying but staring into the sky. Many saw the old man walking through the camp, singing to them as he had by their cribs, putting his finger dripping with honey to the tiny lip. No one doubted that it was a spirit but they were quiet, even the animals, hoping it would walk for the full week among them. Afterwards when we broke camp, pulling up the staves and headed to our separate grazings, there was still silence in the midst of us, neither Jacob nor Esau's sons spoke. They kissed, left each other's cheeks wet, but there were no words, for they feared to break the stillness in which man anticipated his fellow's need and one could still hear the echo of Isaac's voice, watch his ghost glimmering in the night walks.

Now at the door I offer my hand. Take it, O Ancient, take me by another way. Let me taste the honey of thy fingers.

Only slowly we heard as we drifted across the plain, the grunts and moans of the herd, the creaking of the harness, shriek of the birds, all the noise of the world come back into our ears and our voices deafen us.

Eight

"I am lonely," she said.

I wanted to cry.

"Only give it to me."

I was silent but I ached. She would come at me as she had Er, climbing over me in my sleep to thrust her body in among the bright essences with whom I was entangled. "Tamar, Tamar, can we be friends, pals?" I patted her. She shivered.

The first night she showed me the knife marks, a curved white scar across her belly.

"Er's rubbings," I quipped.

My fingers lingered on the ridge of scar, tracing the false womb he had opened in her.

"Touch me," she whispered.

She is not a girl, I realized. There can be no waiting. She took my fingers to her secrecy.

I was eager to explore yet still I shrank. She is not a girl.

The voices do not come to me. They have never come to me. Once I lay in bed and a trembling started. It was like the joy of the images only without me. It started through me and I began to rise. There I hovered above the floor, the spring beginning to bubble in me but I was afraid. I would not let go.

The rope swayed in my hand. I would go up. Never return to that prison of bone, tissue, below. I could look down on the strange body of a boy, his legs akimbo on the bed. Yet where . . .

The moment passed and I settled down upon my form again.

128

So they are dumb but now the spring under my tent is dry too. She lies here, a heavy clod of flesh, obstructing entrance, egress of all that stirring. Am I to search inside her for gates, doors? I tried, I swear, I tried. There was nothing there, a blind tunnel, blocked up.

Yes, she can draw from me something palpable, an embryo, a secret that grows, swells in her, but me?

I hold the seed within myself. At night, I generate.

The sun can not reach me here, hidden deep in the pillows, the blackness draining from the body, bones. I bleach into a jelly, translucent, colorless, no speck of impulse in me. See, let her crawl upon me now, manhandle my privacy, nothing will uplift. I am locked unto myself drinking my body dry.

In the desert there is an old man sitting cross-legged, naked, weeping, holding his hands over his private parts.

Three young men dressed in silks and embroidered cottons are throwing stones at him. They are drunk and laughing. The clothes do not fit them. Five camels wander in circles, their packs spilling out on the sand.

"Who is he?" I ask.

"That old prick," one of the men shouts. He goes up to the elder and snatches his hands away. "Look at that! Disgusting."

"Jump on it," another calls.

"Drop a rock."

"What has he done?" I beg.

One of the men grabs the edge of my robe and rips it pulling me into his face, his bloodshot eyes, his foul breath. "He cut out our eldest brother's heart."

"Why?"

"Why? Why?" they echo mocking. "Why?" they scream at the old man who hides his face from me, ashamed, tear-streaked.

"I heard a voice," he whispers.

They tried to take her from the tent last night. I am too ill, they said, to be her bedfellow. My father says nothing but suspects. Still two sons sick. He will not meet her stare and looks askance. She stays.

I am wicked. I feel it, the evil hoarded, sliding back and forth, quicksilver, in each limb. I withhold myself. The fever makes me sweat it out and I smell myself, rank, sour on the sheets and pillow cases. I stop up my bowels and retain urine in my bladder.

He knew his father was engaged in it, the stillness that settled over the camp, the closed curtains of the tent, his dazed look at the evening meal, for hours afterward.

His brothers would not talk of it. The old man knew what he was doing. Leave him alone.

He stands at the cloth flap of the entrance, pretending to be looking elsewhere.

Hears the moans, the whispers, calls, and suddenly a scream, the ancient one has lost his balance.

He parts the flap. He peeps.

Later he is not sure what he saw.

131

A rod of flesh upright, Noah encircling his own organ, wrapped around it like a vine.

A drunken man lying in vomit with a shriveled penis.

His father, suspended in midair, his white body glowing as he falls through darkness, the face a mask of horror.

A snake, its mouth forced open into which the old man has thrust his head.

Enormous bowels.

Fish, the stench of rotting fish.

A winy sea overwhelmed them, hiss as the black gas burst between their toes and ice fell in blocks from heaven, the ark rolling over and over, spinning down, down, Noah revolving at the tiller.

Remember the hammer of the rain?

Remember the cry of the beasts on board, the lashings of the monster's tail as he writhed caught in the workings of the rudder?

The darkness deep and sticky.

The ice in which they stuck.

The sleep that settled over everything but Noah.

The day he woke them.

Where are the rest?

Gone.

Where?

Noah shook his head, pointed down, up. I'm searching, he said, shrugging his shoulders.

Who did this?

Noah shrugged again.

Who created us?

Noah's hands grasp the air trying to fashion an answer.

How?

Noah grins, points to himself.

Let's look.
Why?
Make me. Make me again.

A white mushroom, creamy, rises out of the ruby ocean.
It is a solid block of sugar, its crown sitting on a tapered neck.

Noah's mouth, enormous, his lips like purple vulvae are coming down on it, swallowing the crown.

Ham begins to back out. Another moment of this and his veins will turn to salt.

Noah is tipping, the thing in his mouth, about to . . .

It is Ham who screams.

Afterward, Shem and Japeth come in, walking backward, holding the blanket between them.

The angel's hand on Jacob's thigh.

Ham had seen his father pee a dozen times. What was the fuss?

"He saw what Ham had done to him."

Ham's mouth.

He tells his brothers.

My father takes my hand. He is afraid to say what is on his mind. "Please don't show me this way," he asks.

"It is myself I am showing!" I answer. "My nakedness."

"No," he says. "It is mine. You are mine. Mine."

slime

"What did you do to me?"

"I looked . . ."

"You are a beast," he muttered.

"I . . ."

"A beast," he said, slowly, solemnly. "That is your burden. Carry it."

135

"Lot, Lot was drunken too. And his daughters uncovered him."

"They were ashamed. The palm leaves, the fig, to hide it."

"What were they hiding, what?"

Jacob threw up his hands, he could not explain. "There is a secret there. If you look it disappears. Hide it. Hide it. It will be sacred."

"Why?"

"Onan," he whispered. "You are not a beast. You are aware. Take that away, it is nothing. Make yourself aware. Hide. Refrain. It will come to you."

"What did he do?"

"He looked."

It was afterward, when Shem and Japeth dropped the blanket that he felt it. Awful, a flame went through him, not only his cheeks but his whole body in a blush that made the tips of his hair start up, his scalp burn; his heart stoked, flaring with it almost to bursting, the heat in his arteries, scalding, going through his groin, unstringing his kneecaps, soft and molten, melting wax in that scarlet fire . . . shame . . . shame . . . he felt such shame.

Beast?

That earth, alive with pestilence, dripping blood, sweating seed, each crumb of it sweet with the perfume of generation. I coddled it in my hands like a potter, formed a mouth in it which cried and spoke to me, fashioned ears to hear my thoughts, breasts between my fingers, legs, calves, thighs, a buttocks and its cleft to receive me. I pressed it to me. An earth corrupt and articulate as my own flesh. Yea, the ground under me was skin and bone and I lay down and was one with it. And when I arose again I was shaped anew.

O Father. Father!

Stories

Mourner

*Magnified and sanctified be His great
name in the world which He has created
according to His will. May He establish
His kingdom during your life and during
your days and during the life of all
the house of Israel, even speedily and at
near time, and say you, Amen.*

—Hebrew Prayer Book

The hand lay like a corpse on the table. It was a gnarled claw, wasted to the bones in a fist as tight as *rigor mortis*. It lay still on the rickety oak table, the flat ribbons of the veins so close to the skin that it seemed as if the flesh had been washed away by time and its blood dried blue and purple on the bone.

Nothing was in its grip. It did not stir an inch.

Across the wooden surface, facing the clenched, unmoving hand, a long ragged fingernail at the end of a gigantic finger scratched back and forth on the splinters of oak.

At the top of the table, four nimble fingers, pale white, wrinkled, drummed and drummed, occasionally twitching sideways with arthritis.

At the very end of the table, opposite the four dancing joints, a fat thumb rocked peacefully.

"A *shandeh!*" cried Rappowitz as his corpse of a hand leaped into the air, the emaciated fist bursting into fingers, four curling nails clawing the air.

For a few seconds the hand beat alone. Dust and its soft fall were heard in the room. Dust was thick as earth in the reading room of the old Orthodox Synagogue. Bright sunshine pouring through the windows of the ancient chamber grew spotted and faded; its rays fell sluggishly through the room; darkening, they nodded sleepily, slowly meandering, flecks, floating to the floor, illuminating a nose, an ear, a finger, in the late afternoon.

All that room, even the stale air, slept in the dust. As if one of Job's shards had been shattered over all, dry dung descended. Dust mantled the shoulders of the four figures, its soft fall.

Listen! The breath of Chomollofsky the giant returns. His wind scrapes the hoarse bellows in his throat. Muzzel's

142

drunken snore, half a sigh, half a song, sings against the window in an echo. One of the four fingers of Tsinger taps on the board, snaps in the air, and at last the actor cries, "A *shandeh* and a *charpeh!*"

The four figures stirred. It was a cue.

The five curling fingers in the air froze. They gripped an imaginary thing. "Shkootz!" shrieked Rappowitz. And he hurled it from his hand. He hurled it with the one-time force of Chomollofsky. It burst from his palm with the power of David's sling, spun through the chamber, smashed the window, going right through the hole, and flying across the street, shattered the foreheads of Shkootzim all over Roxbury. Shkootzim black and white lay dead on the pavements and the Police had to cart them away by the hundreds. One stone! One stone!

And that stone lay on the floor right under Rappowitz's nose. The stone that had come through the identical hole in the window, ten minutes ago. A stone that had the nerve to fly into a holy chamber and bruise the cheek of the giant Chomollofsky, which had never in its eighty years endured such a thing. A stone thrown in the sacred hours of the Shalosh Sudoth!

The stone issued forth out of a group of screaming children, one or two white faces but mostly black. It had come through a window washed by the green waves of time, worn thin as a cheap crystal, stained in a yellowing hue. The stone put its fist through the glass and tore a path through the ghostly flesh of Chomollofsky's huge cheek. The old men stared at the drops of blood that oozed like tears slowly shedding from the wound.

"Police! Police!" screamed Rappowitz through the hole at the mob of excited, demons. Laughter shook a few more

143

shreds of glass from the sieved pane as the children leaped up and down. The Police were a thousand blocks away. The Police had sworn never to come near the neighborhood again. The Police were further away than they had been in the last pogrom of Kiev. The Boston Police made an oath in blood never to come into that part of Dorchester forever.

So it was a miracle. A siren out of nowhere. Right on the last foolish shout, "Police!" It scattered the gang with enough rocks in their hands to stone all to death. Like a handful of pebbles the sound flung children from block to block, scattering before it. Yet the old men didn't even look through the hole to see the ambulance go by. They stared at the giant Chomollofsky's cheek.

It made them sick. Blood! Blood! A plague of Egypt.

Blood now bloomed on the white cheek of Chomollofsky as if he were being slaughtered for the First Born. From the depths of his seven-foot frame, more blood had bubbled up than the doctors at Beth Israel could have suspected. A pint washed away under the table before the silk bandage of a threadbare prayer shawl clotted the cut. The blood ran its fingers down the length of the shawl and caked in the bunched folds against his cheek.

With his free hand, Chomollofsky waved Tsinger back to his seat. He didn't want an ambulance for a cut, a nick. He didn't want the butchers from City Hospital or the bills from Beth Israel. He didn't want a cubicle at the Hebrew Home for the Aged. He wanted to sit at the Shalosh Sudoth and speak as a scholar.

Yet for ten minutes, no one said a word.

It was the Shalosh Sudoth. It was time for ten thousand words. It was time for the deeds of Rabbi Yohan Ben Zakkai, who supported all Israel in his old age, to come and shake the

144

foundations of the Synagogue. It was the hour of Rabbi Akiba, his twenty-four thousand students, and his faithful wife. It was time to talk of clean and unclean, and Rabbi Eleazer, whose opinion the Almighty supported in the Schoolhouse, causing trees to fall, rivers to run backward, the walls to incline, His own voice to trumpet forward, and all to no avail because the other Rabbis were stubborn that day. It was that moment when *Talmud* was to burst the dam of time and rushing forward, choked with a thousand anecdotes bubbling up and down in the text, stories, jokes, gossip, risqué remarks, carry them off two thousand years to the golden halls of Sepphoris and Nehardea.

Amalek had left them speechless. Amalek was out in the street, that gang of Shvartzas and Goyim. For two decades and more, the Goyim of Codman Square had threatened the Temple. Erie Street behind the Synagogue, its Jewish hoodlums, had blocked the way. On a Saturday in the old days, the fists and threats of Erie had been jealous for the honor of the Schul. Not so much as a car came down the street to disturb its prayers. Men of the earth, but their shoulders were the foundation of the Temple.

The pious ignoramuses were removed from the back seats of the Temple. It was appointed that they earn money. Into their hovels, onto their crumbling porches, and up their back steps, smelling of garbage, came others. Little dark children began to hang around the Schul doors, coming up to the old men, tugging at their coats and suit jackets. At first they seemed cute. The parents were well behaved. Solomon sings, "black but comely." Our father, Moses, married a Cushite.

These moved on. And another crowd came in behind. With strange caps on their heads—Egyptians? Torn jerseys, filthy pants, lounging all day, up and down the sidewalks. Trouble

145

came with them. Sticks and stones. A knife or a razor. The old Rabbi from Roxbury's Rooshashah Schul walked home one night through the park. Why not? Was it Poland? Was it Germany? A mild man, a scholar, his throat was cut and his body tossed in the bushes.

All around, up to the very sills of the Synagogue windows, was a sea of black faces. The building was deserted. They promoted the *shummus* to Rabbi. He was never around though. A *minyan* was a thing of the past. The street outside was too dangerous to walk.

Four was no magic number. Why did they stay? Here they were nothing.

Anywhere else they were dirt. Dirt! Dirt!

Seven feet of Chomollofsky was bent in two. He was a hospital case. He wasn't the Chomollofsky who had sent peasants twice his weight tumbling into the rivers of Poland, a barge captain who loaded up in Odessa with a fortune of goods and poled up the streams of Russia, drawing a crew behind him till muscles bulged like ship's knots on his arms. He wasn't the Chomollofsky whose name was inscribed on the marble tablets in the hallway as the Synagogue's Treasurer, year after year, giving his money away in America, money that didn't flow back into his pockets each year as the rivers rose. Chomollosfsky came over a rich man and stayed to be a pauper. The Community that was supposed to take care of him had disappeared. His name was only on the lips of the tablet in the hallway.

Chomollofsky sat with his face clotted to the prayer shawl toward Tsinger. The giant's long finger scratched the table.

Silence. . . What could the former have said to the latter?

What could you say to Tsinger, the old Song and Dance man who had tapped his way from Vilna to Boston nonstop.

146

Tsinger, the *Talmud chochem* of Yiddish Burlesque, whose bones like an ox on the way to the altar were hobbled with arthritis: Tsinger, whose hooves had danced upside down on the curtains across Europe and America; Tsinger was now doing a slow shuffle to the grave.

"Tsinger, sing to us!" Croon to us in that voice you used to have, when the violins stopped, that little tenor that tingled in the crystal streamers of the chandeliers, till the balconies shed tears and the Theatre filled with light; as Eleazer ben Arak sang of mystical things to his master Yohanan on their journey till fire was drawn down from Heaven and the trees of the field flamed, bursting forth into song, and rainbows shot across the sky. The yellow leaf of Angels, their wings, beat the air. "Ascend! Ascend!" cried a voice. And all were drawn up to Heaven for a banquet.

"Ashes and blotten. . . ashes and blotten. . ." muttered Chomollofsky, laying the clotted prayer shawl down on the dark table. "Go home to die," he mumbled, trying to pick himself out of the chair. He was too weak. He leaned back to collect his strength. No one had noticed. The creaking seat, however, broke the silence.

"Rabba . . ." It was Rappowitz speaking. Rappowitz who had been standing, staring ahead as if the rock he had flung, rebounding, struck him senseless, Rappowitz, now picking his eyes up from the stone on the floor, ". . . Rabba said, 'Death, it was no more than the prick of a cupping bowl.' "

The room was absolutely quiet. Along the shelves of the chamber, bowed like ailing spines, decaying musty volumes, fly-spotted refugees from the lost yeshivas of Europe weighed and pondered the remark in the humus of their pages.

For a moment the boards creaked.

147

Again, all was still. Bits of parchment and leather crumbled at the edge of books, splintering into the dust of the air, filling the room with decay, its odor. In the great hall next to the reading chamber, there were cobwebs under the seats. Rappowitz knew. He had been in there in the morning. The Rabbi showed up, saw, said, "No *minyan*," smiled, and walked out. What could you do? It was the law. The ark was full of moldering scrolls. The good ones had been carried away to Newton.

The Synagogue was wealthy. Don't worry! Only the money was in Newton where they had put up another building and there was a waiting list three blocks long to get in. Out there, this morning, the parking lot was filled with Cadillacs and Lincoln Continentals. If they had wanted to, they could have sent a Chrysler station wagon or two, into Dorchester. Israel was full of deceptions. Rappowitz was willing to stretch a point, to overlook. There were supposed to be black Jews in the world. Why didn't they show up?

Rappowitz had been out to Newton for a look. There was nothing there. It wasn't a House of Study. It was a Community Center, a Rumpus Room, a Country Club, and there was a two thousand dollar initiation fee to get in.

Better to sit in the cobwebs, the Saturday afternoons of the past. The Shalosh Sudoth when he was President! Before the Crash, in the days of his sock factory. He still had the boxes in his house and door to door, he eked out a living selling moth-eaten socks. Rappowitz pushed the socks to the back of his mind. The room was filling up with the past. Orthodox came from all over America to listen in. There were dialecticians who could shame the Rabbis of Pumbeditha with their wit, argument, scholarship. The voices of controversy over a learned point shattered the panes in their frames.

The gold bole of the sun flashed through the hole in the window, stinging his eyes. Now they had only his memory, Chomollofsky rarely spoke, Muzzel snored. . .

The Synagogue in Dorchester couldn't go on much longer. Soon boards would cross the door. For two months there had been no *minyans* for Shabbos. Three men died, two moved away, and one could no longer come. Tsinger wasn't regular in his attendance. There was no one coming into the neighborhood. Only one sure thing. Rappowitz looked across the room at the rise and fall of a purple nose, Muzzel, whose Yiddish nickname, "Lucky," was borne out by experience. The drunken waddle gave him immunity from attack. Eighty years old and he outdrank the hippo in the Franklin Park Zoo. He was never late to services. A bottle of rye, scrupulously provided, assured his prompt attendance. An agreement had been made, a glass at the beginning, two at the end.

The drunk's breath grew heavier and shook the dust in a cloud above his nose. A Shalosh Sudoth!

"And Raba said also. . ." It was Chomollofsky, in an ashen whisper. " 'No more than a hair picked out of a bowl of milk.' "

Tsinger roused himself. He sat up in his chair, clicking his thumb against his forefinger. "It reminds me of a joke in *Mo'Ed Katon*. The Angel of Death met Rabbi Shesheth in the marketplace and requested his soul. 'Please,' said Rabbi Shesheth. 'Not in the marketplace! Let's go home and talk about it.' "

Rappowitz smiled, adding, "Yet Rabbi Nahman asked

Raba on his deathbed, 'You know him, nu? Tell him to leave you alone.' What did Raba say?"

"Aaaaaah," gurgled Tsinger, remembering. Rappowitz beat him to it.

" 'Since I lost my muzzel, he doesn't listen to me.' "

Muzzel in the corner awoke. *"Nu?* Time for trinks?" he asked with a hopeful grin, seeing their smiles.

"Time for some muzzel," quipped Tsinger.

"It's always time for muzzel," the drunk responded gaily.

"We were speaking of Death," said Rappowitz, souring.

"A serious subject," said Muzzel, still smiling, "What did you decide?"

"A hair. . ." They could barely hear Chomollofsky. His frame nodded, a crumbling oak, over the table.

"I remember that passage," Rappowitz said. He brought his hand up to his forehead, sealed his eyes. Swaying, he turned away from Muzzel and began to recite, mumbling out the Aramaic of the commentary in Yiddish. "Raba was at the bed of Rabbi Nahman. He saw Nahman shake, grow rigid, stretching into the arms of Death. 'Tell him to stop!' cried Nahman. 'He squeezes me.'

" 'Aren't you highly regarded?' asked Raba.

" 'Who is regarded, who is esteemed, who is distinguished before the Angel of Death?'

"As Nahman died, Raba whispered, 'Show yourself to me.'

"So in a dream, one night, Nahman came.

" 'Master, did you suffer pain?'

" 'No more than taking a hair from the milk. Yet. . .' "

He paused, his voice heavy, " 'Were the Holy One, blessed be He, to say to me, Go back to the world as you were, I wish it not. . .'

" 'The fear of death is too great.' "

The snap of a twig. Tsinger's fingers. "There's a joke."

The men bent forward to hear, all but Chomollofsky, who was already in that position, his head almost resting on the table.

"The Angel of Death comes to Rabbi Ashi in the marketplace. Out of nowhere he appears and says. . ." Tsinger crooked his finger. Nasty and confidential, the Angel coughed in Tsinger's soprano, " 'Let's go!'

" 'Hold on.' " It was Rabbi Ashi, palm upraised. " 'I got to arrange my notes. You want a disgrace in Heaven? Let me have thirty days.'

"At the end of thirty days comes the Angel.

" 'Let's go!'

" 'What's the hurry?'

" 'Your successor, Rabbi Hunah, is waiting for your place.' "

Tsinger looked around the room. An old joke.

"As for Rabbi Hisda," Rappowitz rocked back and forth, faster and faster. "He could never overcome him. Hisda's mouth was always full, Torah . . . Torah . . . Torah . . . The Angel climbed into a tree, a cedar over the Schoolhouse. The trunk snapped—"

A skull hit the table. No one heard. Rappowitz had clapped his hands.

"Hisda stuttered. His soul was snatched."

"Ah," said Muzzel. "You know of Rabbi Hiyya?" The drunk wet his lips' "Such a man! A real *chochem*! When he died, fiery stones fell out of the sky. *Gevult*! So pious, the Devil could never get near him. What to do, the poor fellow is scratching his brains. Going *meshuggeh*. At last, he gets an idea. He dressed up like a *shnorrer*, rags, dirty. He comes to Hiyya's house, knocks on the door, asks for a trink."

151

"Food! He asks for food," Rappowitz interrupted, banging the table.

"For you it's food. I got to have a trink."

"Let him have a drink," said Tsinger.

"He asks for a trink," Muzzel continued. "A glass of schnapps. And they bring it to him. It's a pious household. But the Shnorrer shouts in, 'Nu, Hiyya, you despise the thirsty?' "

"The poor," cried Rappowitz.

"The poor are thirsty," drawled Tsinger.

Muzzel rose in his patched gray overalls. A torn golfing cap was pushed back on his head. His huge brown face tanned in the gutters of Boston shone with the fire of a life of hard liquor. His shadow, dark and swollen, rolled on the wall. Bloodshot, his eyes gleamed.

He shouted, lost in the story, "Hiyya was ashamed! He came to the door himself. He had a glass in his hand and peeked out at the *shnorrer. Nu!* at that moment, the *shnorrer* pulls out an iron bar, glowing, hot red."

The drunk's fist shook. It burst into flames.

The sun setting behind the broken windows of the ancient chamber burned like a bed of coals and crimsoned the sky, hissing in the sound of a death rattle. Scarlet light filled the room. The old men were struck senseless. Dust fell and fell in the silence, collecting on the lids, in the hollowing sockets, of Chomollofsky's eyes.

O breath where have you fled, out of our roofs and tenements, out of our holy books, over the shattered glass, the crumbling wall, our community, the soul of the boatman ascends.

A Sanhedrin of corpses. The Mourners begin the Kaddish, *Magnified and sanctified be His great name.* . . .

Milky Way

Sol Hershey's face loomed white, lonely, a moon above the hurly-burly milky way of Fourteenth Street, crowded constellations of midtown shoppers petering out as the broad New York thoroughfare spanned Ninth Avenue and his dark unhappy window stacked with dusty decaying foods.

Sol!

I stumbled into three ladies, their arms full of fruits, groceries, lingerie, stopping short, surprised at those pale round cheeks of Hershey's rising behind the glass.

So Sol was back. I was party to the agony looking from the wrinkled pillars of the New York Sunday *Times*, last week's; a slight body, middle-aged paunch, his white T-shirt stretching as he leans staring at some distant point in the sky.

I, a stranger, one of the family, unknown to Sol. An accident, one day, sipping my coffee with rye toast, I heard the first words, a story was taking place in the drab space of the luncheonette, domestic tragedy, real stuff.

153

It started, a breath, a sigh. Mrs. Hershey, one hand on the cash register ringing up a lettuce and tomato, the other trying to spread cream cheese on a roll, her eyes on the little boy who hovered over the candy boxes, a filcher from the Bowling Lanes next door.

"Hey, you want it or not?" she snapped, losing her patience as the boy's hand grazed the box tops, craning his neck horribly to the side, trying to see if he was watched. A pile of cups in the sink crashed over; the cook had given up dish washing. The filcher fled with fingers stuck to a Tootsie Roll. "Hey! Hey!" Mrs. Hershey cried, afraid to leave the cook with the cash register. The lettuce and tomato was on the floor. Cream cheese registered on the keys as she rang up the other sandwich, slammed two slices of white bread into the toaster and started slicing the tomato again with a heavy breath.

Heavy? I couldn't go back to my pages in the *Times*. And one of the neighborhood ladies, a well-dressed one from the Luxury Co-op, in for morning tea, leaned over the counter.

"Where's your husband?"

First you have to know that Mrs. Hershey was not unattractive. An immigrant, I guessed—the slight Hungarian accent. She had beautiful black hair, a girl's, long, tied in a bun so as not to pick up grease spots everywhere. She was close to forty, maybe, but still pretty. The Polish cook, whose face was mottled, raspberries, smacked his lips, scraping the grill, muttering about dumb dames. Recent events were causing him to assert himself. Her legs were good. I had seen that once as she stretched to stack magazines on the top rung of the wall rack. Mrs. Hershey's face, sometimes woeful, then smiling, alive yet, not the usual counter drab's, an iron brace on her lips. The last few times I had come in she watched me, covertly, a flattering attention.

"Gone," she whispered, a slice of the bleeding love apple, the end of her breath, falling to the side.

"Oh yeah," the Co-op Lady broke into a broad smile, cracking the make-up in her cheeks.

The knife slammed down, a wafer-thin heart toppled feathery to the butcher board.

"Where is he?"

The toast popped. Mrs. Hershey slapped a bed of lettuce on the bottom half.

"I told you."

"Come on. No kidding."

"Gone." She looked up as she shoveled the sandwich to the side, her eyes indignant; black brows raised as if to ask, "Who ever heard of this? What's going on?"

"You're making a joke, huh?"

The neighbor taps the table, a feeble comic beat. Only Mrs. Hershey is mumbling no, her bandless hand plunged into the sink, two days' dirty dishes. I measure time in this midden heap. "He's gone. Left."

Sol Hershey has abandoned his Hungarian beauty, survivor of Dachau, in a mass grave. A Ninth Avenue luncheonette. In the background I hear the cook, his knife grating the hot fat off the griddle. A lover of bacon.

So the melancholy Sol, that peanut of a man, whose flabby build seemed a natural for the slow gas jet of a luncheonette, had made a break and run. The *New York Times* rustled in my hands, in the excitement, I lost a few of the bitter words that Mrs. Hershey had addressed to the churning waters of the sink as the Luxury Co-op pumped. I

155

was racing Sol to California with three weeks' receipts and the tax money. A fleeing Mustang, a black beauty, radio blaring, and a Puerto Rican girl sliding passionately on the shiny leatherette by his side. Sol, a blank checkbook and forged credit cards, his bald white head tanning as he whoops it up at the Holiday Inn, cavorting in their swimming pools. Sol squeezing lemons in the slot machines, Reno, Las Vegas; a flood of silver, poker-faced Hershey.

He had it in him. I remembered now, the time he took on a whole crowd waiting for the bus by Ninth Avenue. The usual bunch of riffraff, Italians, Blacks, Spanish, a gang from the Bowling Lanes, wise asses, a few Ukrainian delinquents for good measure. It started to rain and Sol went out to put canvas over his papers and magazines. A fat lady was leaning on them. He couldn't tug the cover over. He asked her to move. She told him where to get off, a few filthy words and her kids chimed in. A nurse, her mouth had an enema in it, half the bus stop was related to her too. They crowded around, wouldn't move either. Jeers, bad noises, they're calling him kike, Yid, Jew bastard, honkie! The rain is coming down hard and they push under the green-striped awning, jostle him away from his papers, laughing. "I tole him off, didn' I, uh?"

A lesser man than Sol would have slunk back in and sulked behind the counter. He walked in his door and came right back out with a steel pole. The rain is slashing down and Sol, brandishing the shaft over the surprised crowd, hooks it to the awning and rolls up green and white stripes on them. No more cover from his store. Let them stand drenched under the open skies, and before they realize what's up, he's back in, locking the door behind him. Oh, he's smart. He doesn't

156

thumb his nose through the glass windows. No point in provoking them to smashing. He just putters about the candy boxes in an absent-minded way, tasting the sweets.

So I could see him on the beach at Santa Monica, black hair curling on his chest. Muscles bulge on his arms. The starlets wriggle round Sol the Surf.

Meanwhile, back at Hershey's luncheonette, I lean across the counter like the Bear, Ursa Major. "It follows I am rough and lecherous." The Little Dipper is sparkling in my head. Mrs. Hershey has begun to show me favors. She has remarked upon my hand-embroidered *taliss* bag. I have explained—in mourning for my mother. A sigh, deep, motherly, those dark eyes. Capricorn the horned goat kicks up his heels. I can almost reach over the chrome plungers of the fountain, cherry, vanilla, and touch her sympathetic breasts. She makes me an egg cream and I can hear the fizz set a thousand bubbles going in the sweet syrup, milky. The atmosphere, the air between us is agitated, so her eyes are twinkling. She undercharged me a nickel for the drink. I'm in her hire, a gigolo.

After all, the world is agog. "These late eclipses in the sun and moon . . . love cools." Sol must have been reading the sex magazines, his racks. The *National Enquirer*, wife-poisoners, stranglers. Where else would the notion to flee enter his balding middle-aged head? I sneak a peek, too, although it's hard with Mrs. Hershey's maternal eye on me. That stuff is for the trash waiting for buses. Yet who knows what goes on after hours, those honeyed drinks she mixes me? Plenty of time when the door is shut, locked up for the night, to raid the shelves of dirty books. Now that Sol has left, she must be curious.

At night I remove my *yarmulke* and dream of Mrs. Hershey. She comes knocking at the door of my tiny three-room flat.

"I brought you a malted," she says, coming over to the narrow bed. I take the frothy chocolate drink, its chill aluminum container.

"Are you a good Jewish boy?"

I nod, trying to smile sweetly. "You miss her?"

I nod. And Mrs. Hershey unties the string that holds her glossy flood of black. It tumbles down as her fingers pluck the bone button from the hole at the top of her fountain blouse. Another and another and then the catch, little machine at the back of her brassiere so I can see as she lets it fall the globes of comfort she has brought.

"You need more."

I barely move my head up, embarrassed to indicate, yes. Only Mrs. Hershey, smiling, undoes the side buttons of her skirt. She hangs it neatly on the chair, takes off her half-slip. Shows it to me. "Pretty."

I cannot speak but I admire the lace frill along the pink silk. She pats my cheek, sits, a kind look in her eye for me, waiting a while so I won't be afraid. We smile at each other.

"My panties are nice too." She stands up and slowly pushes the elastic band around her tummy down over her hips, her thighs, her knees. I see the black bush, the milky body, and dizzily an ivory form sways, tears in my eyes as she comes over to me on the bed, takes my pajamas off, cradles me, turning me over in her arms so that I rest on her breasts, then fall into the deep, musky sweetness, sliding down into the whole, oh

We lie back on the blue *taliss* bag, its gold embroidery. The thick plush-velvet pillow is stuffed with soft silk prayer

158

shawls. Mrs. Hershey has taken out the black phylactery boxes, their long straps, and bound us together, winding the endless strips of inky leather around our naked torsos. The prayer boxes cover our private parts. And she murmurs the invocation as I wake, looking into her beautiful eyes. "I will betroth you to myself forever. I will betroth you to myself . . . in kindness and in mercy. I will betroth you to myself in faithfulness: and you shall know. . . ." I wind her hair, raven locks, around my fingers. In my palm the tresses form the holy name.

Meanwhile, the fat is frying at the luncheonette. The Polish cook has noticed. He is getting nasty. My rye toast is burned. He slaps it down on the counter and tries to spill the coffee in my lap. Mrs. Hershey rushes to me to tidy up. Her rag flashing by the plastic top, she forces napkins on me for my pants, offers to take back the toast. Embarrassed by the Pole, her eyes are sad, helpless. The red clusters seethe in the Short Order's face. Assert yourself, I think. Only she is quicker, coming around with a glass of water to daub out the stains. Deftly, with delicate pats, drawing the rich color of coffee from gray Dacron pants. Bending to me as I sit, breathless, without a motion on my stool. The cook is steaming through his nose. I am going to spin with her, round and round and round. The seat creaks.

She flushes, withdraws her hand. Too slow though, I am sure, too slow. Oh, I will wait. The Polack glares, his face enflamed, flaring, the red comb of a cock. I can wait, I think. Oh, foolish heart.

Yes, Sol is back, pensive, stooped, staring into the dusk, waiting for the first faint star. His face, a ghost, no traces of Catalina. Perhaps he fled no farther than Canarsie, headed East instead of West, toward a sister or brother, reaching the

159

sea at Rockaway, gray, tired sands, old ladies propped on canes, in wheelchairs, saw his fate, returned, resigned. Blinded, he stretches, his belly showing under his undershirt, between two pillars of the news. Only he has played Delilah.

Sol is back, but they do not meet. She by morning. He by afternoon—and that irregular. See, I have been watching, passing, repassing, stealthily, twice a day. A bag of religious articles tucked under my arm. Magic.

There is a story here and I am gathering its pieces.

Shpippik

Here in the city man dies oppressed at heart, man perishes with despair in his heart. I have looked over the wall and I see the bodies floating on the river . . ."

The Epic of Gilgamesh

1.

Chaim Shpippik put his finger in his nose. A long bony finger, he pushed it up until the top tickled his sinus. He drew in a deep breath, exhaled gently pushing the finger out and wiped it back and forth under his nostril.

"Aaaaah . . ." he sighed, bobbing back and forth as if in the synagogue.

A cold March, Chaim, bundled in a green army jacket, sat in the hut on 14th Street, a belt of silver slung around his waist,

161

wondering when spring would, at last, come. The canvas flapped at his back, wind whistled through the cracks, no one was interested in the news, weather, nothing. The gossip of four continents was piled high in Shpippik's shack. Shpippik slept on it, his head leaning on disasters, outrages, incredible disclosures; customers silently left their dimes and slipped the bulletin out from under his nose, nostril hairs tickling the facts, stubble of his cheek scraping at them.

Facts were nonsense to Shpippik. His own life made no sense.

Thirty years ago, facts were done for, he was through with them. He sold them but he slept on them, snoozed on them, snored on them, let his nose dribble all over—let the customers think what they want.

2.

Meanwhile the winds howled around Shpippik, a black gust full of cinders tore at the tent cords of his canvas, whistled through the cracks of his booth, threatened to upend the fragile box of slats tied to the sidewalk, dump it off. Shpippik and his house were only a step above the gutter.

The tin clattered on the sides, hooks, nails, hinges, that held the thing together, trembled, shaking its shelves, even the bench under Shpippik swayed but the master snorted on through the storm that soaked his slippers as waves broke against the box's sides, slid under the threshold, coal barges crashed against the Con Edison docks three blocks away, sheets of water pinned pedestrians in the doorways, cars stalled in the street, while Lear with shaven beard, resigning anger, slept behind the drawn curtain of his canvas under the constant sun of a single bright electric bulb.

162

3.

Shpippik is no king. An adept, a Baal Shem, hovering on the edge of the abyss, contemplating . . .

At the lip of Manhattan, Shpippik nods back and forth, up and down.

Says Levi Isaac from Berditshev — "Some serve . . . with human intellect . . . others . . . gaze is fixed on Nothing . . . who is granted this . . . loses the . . . intellect, but . . . returns . . ."

Levi!

" . . . returns . . . such contemplation . . . intellect, he finds it full . . . divine and inflowing splendor."

Levi! Shpippik has not returned.

Does he see his family, the seven heavens, the holy fire, self-consuming, German gas jets, copper spigots, golden candlesticks?

I, his disciple, who have watched him shuffle from the luncheonette after a single cup of coffee, affirm he has transcended all details.

You can dance before his newsstand, pee on his counter, stick your fingers in his eyes. The body is slumped worthless, while his spirit wanders.

4.

The mysteries of Shpippik.

His organ?

No one has ever seen it in extended form.

Slack in his pants, it curls in upon itself, heavy as a watermelon, unrolled at least three feet. If one could stiffen, summon it to attention, fertility would burst upon the city.

A billion Shpippiks endowed with specks of their father's light, male and female, would fly against the sun.

Shpippik triumphant! Shpippik would penetrate every nook and cranny. Flowers of his making springing from every crack in the city's walls.

The blossoms of Shpippik.

Peace upon the earth.

5.

He was not easy to discover. There are many other teachers in the neighborhood, masters of earlier steps. Beryl the shoeman, for instance, who taps furiously on the heels and toes of his customers, beating out the rap that has filled him, escaped from Europe only to have the one daughter killed while crossing the street.

After kissing the other and his mother goodbye as ashes. *Auf Wiedersehen!* His second wife crazy now, Beryl is a professor of the absurd. He pinches everything in sight, male, female, pushes the girls legs up in the air, trying on specials, discounts, reducing prices every inch with his thumb. Is leather consolation? Better carve in the customers' flesh. "No more joy," he barked at me. "No more holidays," he shouted when I wished him—happy Passover. "All over," he whispered in my ear. "For the old country."

Beryl, still using words.

Ernie, further along, opens his lips only for himself, throws a wall of change, plates, forks, knives, at people, dreading the touch of human fingers. Ernie the counterman, a mutterer who denounces the world, hobbling back and forth, hurling dishes at the patrons so that toast, eggs, home fries fall in their laps.

Yes, an army of minor disciples walk the streets past Shpippik's stand, none of them recognizing the disguise.

This city (and its walls) that has so bruised the multitude they walk about with faces black and blue, injured, grotesque, fractured mouths, cheekbones, jaws, knocked all out of shape, Shpippik sleeps. He rises.

6.

To the first heaven of the fiery vision, to which only the devout descend; blue fire licks at the sleeve edge of his tattered coat.

To the second, head first on the counter, singed, smoked, antiseptic, a boiled chicken, he and his garments purified of all human dross.

To the third where a hand plucks in his bowels, at his vocal chords, esophagus, back and forth, eviscerates him. His sincerity a string, the pitch strikes back without a fault.

Down to the fourth, where God himself comes to fill the devotee with terrible and intimate presence so that Shpippik, his bellies, slack flesh, shudders.

And, only a breath away, in the fifth, where the holiness of Shpippik echoes before the Creator, a snore.

Oh the sixth, the place glittering, where Rabbi Akiba warns us not to tarry. And the student without understanding is struck on the head with iron bars by the gate keepers, that goose who imagines waves of the ocean engulfing him, storming, overwhelming, "And there is not a drop of water, only the ethereal glitter of marble plates around the palace. 'What's the meaning of these waters?' The keepers cry, 'Idiot! You can't see? One of those fathers kissed the Golden calf, *nu?* Out, out, *touchus!*' They brain him with bars, 'Not worthy to see the king.' "

165

But the newspaperman, asleep, passes, at the highest stand, faces the Presence, the shape which is only a shimmer, the throne a mere symbol, through the veil in which all the threads of Creation run, even to the secret of the Messiah, and it brushes Shpippik's nose, the curtain, dazed the prayer streams from his praise to the Sublime in the chambers of grandeur. For there are realms beyond the Seven Heavens, as we know, and the body, dissolved in the sweetness of the Maker, may yet refine itself further. Even He, the Almighty, according to a secret doctrine, is engaged. . . .

7.

I know you, fakers, liars—the real world? I spit on it. No hope to animate this mass of flesh, this Shpippik, stiffen its spine, organ. His body rises like dough, yours, mine, a fungus, a rotten tide between the teeth of city windows, jaws of the rooftops, drowning, sinking. I see it. Destroys us all.
Shpippik sleep.
Disturb him ye who dare.

According to a heresy
Of the Optimist Shmatte
Rabbi Abraham—
Since we read descend for ascend
Shpippik did not go up but down
under a million tons
Pre-Cambrian, schist, shale

Shpippik!

166

The whole city
rests
on his
weight
foundations
press
bituminous
Shpippik
slowly
reflects
     d
i   n
a   o
   m

Mark Mirsky was born in Boston and grew up on Blue Hill Avenue which runs through the former towns of Dorchester, Roxbury and old Mattapan. He attended the Boston Public Latin School, Harvard College and Stanford University. He is the editor of *Fiction* and an Assistant Professor of English at The City College of New York.

His stories and articles have appeared in *The New Directions Annual, The Progressive, The Boston Sunday Globe, The New York Sunday Times Book Review, The Washington Post* and *Partisan Review.*

FICTION COLLECTIVE

Books in Print:

Searching for Survivors by Russell Banks

Reruns by Jonathan Baumbach

Museum by B. H. Friedman

The Secret Table by Mark J. Mirsky

Twiddledum Twaddledum by Peter Spielberg

98.6 by Ronald Sukenick

Statements: New Fiction, edited by Fiction Collective Authors